THINK OF THE CITY

as an organism. It lives to protect us, to sustain us. It keeps away the terrors and dangers and discomforts of the Out, and it feeds and clothes us. It provides the air we breathe, the water we require, the food we need. It is never too warm nor too cold . . .

Imagine if you can a world where food depends on the whims of a hostile nature. If men are caught in the open without proper clothing or shelter, they die from too much heat or cold. Many men who have no cities such as ours have died in great pain from weather or disease or wild animals attacking them.

We're protected from all these things. But what we get, we have to pay for. . . .

But while that was true of the all-encompassing City of that colonized planet, was it not also true of any maximum-security prison? If so, was the price to be paid: freedom, truth, progress?

The
CITY
MACHINE

by
Louis Trimble

DAW BOOKS, INC.
DONALD A. WOLLHEIM, PUBLISHER

1301 Avenue of the Americas
New York, N. Y.   10019

First printing 1972

DAWsf
BOOKS

PRINTED IN U.S.A.

I

The late-hour shift was a third gone when the light flashed in the tech room, calling Ryne to Scan Central. He found the four scanmen staring at their screens, watches in hands.

Fuller, the shift head, looked around. "We're all getting the same picture on a ninety-second repeat run."

Ryne moved over and studied Fuller's screen. The grimy streets of Lower City slid across the screen, picked up by the probing eye of the scan camera. At this hour the streets were not only drab but empty. It was too early for Shift Change at the factories; too late for other workers to be up.

A flicker of movement on the left side of Fuller's screen caught Ryne's attention. What had appeared to be a bundle of rags or litter cast aside in a recessed doorway twitched just enough to disturb the shadows in which it lay.

"Hold it," Ryne said.

Fuller reached out to his adjusters, stopping the picture and bringing it to close resolution. Ryne leaned forward, waiting for the sharp focus of the closeup. When it came, he saw that the bundle of rags was an old man, a typical derelict drunk. Ryne wondered where they got their illegal alcohol. He'd lived in Lower City long enough before rising to Upper City and he'd never heard a whisper of the source.

His eyes moved to the other three screens. He should have seen something of each of the four quarters of Lower City, since a different quarter was assigned to each scan.

5

Instead he saw the same scene as Fuller's screen carried—
the same street, the same doorway, the same old man,
every ninety seconds.

"That's enough," Ryne said. "Somebody's playing it
cute and jamming the scanline between Lower City and
here." He moved out of the room and down the hall to
Communication Central. The three late-shift girls were at
their boards, idle at the moment. Linne was in her supervisor's cubicle. She looked up and smiled at him through
the transparent plasti-window.

He went into the cubicle. "Trouble on the scans." He
glanced at her board, noting its inactivity.

Linne said softly, "When you came in, I closed the
lines down. Lean close to me and the girls will think
you're setting up a date."

"I intend to," Ryne said. He bent toward her. "Is this
it? Is this what you told me to look for?"

"This is it," she agreed softly. "The trouble is down
beyond the Central Utilities Core. You'll be met there."

"Before or after I fix the jammed line—or do I fix it?"

"You fix it." She smiled at him gently. "And you'll be
met afterward. We don't want the Coordinator to send
someone down to help you out." Her hand moved to
touch his fingers lightly. "I know you think you've made
your decision, Ryne. But listen to the man who meets
you. Don't really make up your mind until then. Because
once you say 'yes' to them, there's no going back."

She paused and added softly, "If you tried to go back,
it would be the end of us all—of everything we've worked
for."

"I'll listen," Ryne said. "And I'll try to balance the
alternatives, if only out of habit. But I'm a Riser too. I
came from down there, and I had fourteen years of knowing what it's like to be a Lower. If what I hear offers a
chance to really change things, saying no would be
damned hard."

Linne said quietly, "You've also had twelve years of
being an Upper. Twelve years of security and enough to
eat and a decent place to live. Just remember that you'll
be risking all that, risking your whole future life. So don't
say yes just because of me." Her eyes were soft meeting
his. "No one person is worth that much. You have to

believe—down here." She touched her breastbone. "You have to believe as I and the others do."

"I've thought about both sides of it," Ryne said. He took a deep breath to steady himself, to keep from bending forward and kissing her here, to show her somehow the depths of his affection. But that would only make her think he was trying to please her rather than use his own mind to make his decision. He was, she had told him more than once, very susceptible to suggestion. And perhaps it was true. When he was with her, his decision was clear enough; when they were apart and he was alone, the doubts came.

He said again, "I'll listen. I'll think about it. I'll make up my own mind."

She warmed him with her smile. "The girls are beginning to look this way."

Ryne backed to the door. "Then get me the Coordinator on a private line, will you?"

"At this hour? Can't you just go?"

"No," Ryne said. "Not into the utility tunnels without clearance. Besides, I'll need a helper. I can't request one. His office has to."

"The helper is all arranged for," she said. She opened her board and flicked a switch. Ryne crossed to a communicator at the far side of the room. He lifted it and waited, listening for an answer to her call to the top level of Upper City, to the man who alone had the responsibility for Lower and Upper Cities, and the responsibility for coordinating the work they did with those at the very top, the High.

He had never personally talked to the Coordinator, and he felt uneasy when the Coordinator demanded a video hookup on the call. Ryne studied the most familiar face on Upper City viewscreens; it seemed to him he had seen that face and listened to the persuasive voice at least once a day since his rising from Lower City.

Yet this was a different kind of image, a more intimate one; and Ryne thought that the Coordinator was becoming gray and slightly jowly. But he was still tall and erect with the kind of shoulders that had helped him figuratively batter his way through the obstacles that had stood in the way of his becoming the most important man below the High. His eyes were alert, despite his having been wakened after only a short period of sleep.

"Scan Technician Ryne reporting a nonroutine problem," Ryne said formally.

"I'm listening," the Coordinator said.

Ryne saw his eyes drop toward the desk visible at waist level. The Coordinator would have his file there; he was not a man to approach anything unprepared. Ryne said, "The scans have been jammed for a ninety-second repeat. Same picture from all sectors. I'd say the technique used was pretty sophisticated."

"I'm hooked in," the Coordinator said. "I can see what you mean. How do you think it's being done?"

"A holographic film loop set to repeat every ninety seconds," Ryne said promptly. "I think it's been plugged into the system somewhere above the point where all the feeder cables come together but below where the main cable passes through Lower City street level."

"Logical. What do you need to fix it?"

"An assistant to hold the big lamp and a pass into the Core."

"It will be arranged by the time you reach the Core Entry Room." He paused briefly. "Report to me personally on completion."

Ryne was too intent in trying to read something into the Coordinator's tone to guard against his natural tendency toward being sardonic. "If I succeed, that is."

"In either case." The connection was abruptly broken.

Ryne moved back to Linne's cubicle. She said, "Your helper will be a man named Mabton. Remember—just because you've agreed to listen doesn't mean he'll trust you. And the Core isn't the safest place to get into an argument."

"I'll remember," he said. He bent, brushing his lips across her cheek. When he straightened up, he said, "If I'm a little late for tonight's date, don't go running off with someone else."

It was their private joke; in the year since they'd been keeping company, they had reserved themselves exclusively for one another. As he left, he heard one of the girls call softly to Linne, "I wish I had a man willing to snoozle me in public. When are you two going to break down and get a pair-up license?"

A minor flood of calls lighting the boards kept Linne from having to answer. Ryne stood a moment watching the graceful efficiency with which she performed her routine tasks. She was damned attractive to him in a tilt-nosed way. Like himself, she had dark hair and dark eyes, intense against skin tones belonging to a blonde. And while she was slender in contrast to his burliness, she gave no impression of fragility. If anything, he had always found in her a spiritual strength he was not sure that he could match.

He went directly to the next level down, the last before the three-level gap that separated Lower from Upper City. Here a small contingent of the Coordinator's Auxiliaries—his volunteer guards—watched for any Lower who might try to infiltrate from below.

His Core pass was waiting. He went through a doorway as one of the guards pressed a release button. He entered a small room with one wall made up of the great circular side of the Core, the big duct that carried the vital utilities from deep underground into Upper City and on to the High. Beside an open doorway in the Core wall stood a small, wiry man a little older than Ryne. He wore the rough coveralls of a Lower, with a tech-assistant insignia on his sleeve. That meant he either worked for the factory management or for the Wardens themselves; in either case he wouldn't be a man too popular with rank-and-file Lowers.

"Mabton," he said, not offering to shake hands. He had one of the big lamps beside him, and he bent, slipping the straps of the power pack onto his shoulders. When they had fixed the helmet lamps on their heads, Mabton said, "Who goes first?"

"I do," Ryne said dryly. "If you slip I won't feel as much as you would if I fell on you."

Mabton grinned sourly. "Don't slip, not on the ladders. It's a long way down in some places." He moved aside to let Ryne go first.

The Core was a mass of tubes and cables running up the center of a great duct. Ladders allowed vertical movement, and where the Core ran level with the cross section of the City, narrow catwalks allowed slow progress. There was no light except that from the bulbs in their headlamps.

They went down slowly, carefully, the only sounds their steadying breathing and the scrape of soft boot soles on the plasti-metal rungs of the ladder. At the first cross section, Mabton stepped onto the platform and eased the weight of the power pack from his shoulders. "How far down do we go?"

"I was expecting you to tell me," Ryne said with soft sarcasm.

Mabton threw him a sour grin. "I was hoping to detour and tap one of the hydroponic-food-factory storerooms. Us Lowers can always use an extra mouthful."

Ryne made no answer. He recalled only too clearly his own days as a Lower. There had never been quite enough food to stretch even a young child's small belly; and a growing boy was always hungry. The most impressive discovery he had made on first rising had been that Uppers ate three full meals a day and, if they chose, could even buy additional food from their earnings. He had heard that the Highs ate whenever and whatever they pleased; but even after years in Upper City he found that hard to believe.

"I didn't mean to step on a sensitive toe," Mabton gibed into the silence.

"No pain," Ryne said shortly. "I was wondering how a small man with an empty belly could carry that power pack." He turned from Mabton's challenging grin to the ladder.

"We should be about Lower City level now," Ryne said. He struggled to bring back sharply the schematic he had carefully memorized. "In a few more meters, the Core should be running through Warden Central. Below its basement floor, the main branch ducts begin coming in."

"No problem, then," Mabton said. "Just find the duct carrying the communication cables and follow it."

"Except that the entire duct doesn't feed into the Core," Ryne answered. He climbed slowly downward, talking as he went. "Only the cables themselves feed in. That means we have to go all the way to Utilities Central and backtrack to get into the communications duct itself. It'll be a long haul through a number of side ducts."

"I'll survive," Mabton said.

They were silent again. Another fifty meters downward and the big Core made a direct right-angle turn. Now they could follow the horizontal catwalk, and they made better time. Suddenly it angled again, once more downward. And here was another cross-sectional plate, allowing them to leave the ladder.

"This should be Utilities Central," Ryne said. There was a door in the curving side of the Core. He opened it and led the way into a cavernous room that echoed emptily with the shuffling sounds from their boot soles.

They stepped onto the wide flat top of a great cylinder that stretched meters in all directions. The Core ran through its center, and around the outer perimeter of the Core sat a large number of metallic boxes.

Ryne said, "Let's break and take the weight of my lunch out of my tool kit." He sat down, some distance from the wall of the Core, and opened the kit.

"Aren't you afraid of the radiation?" Mabton gibed. But he seated himself next to Ryne.

"We're supposedly screened from radiation—whatever that is."

He passed Mabton one of his two small food packets and extended his flask of synkaf. "If you don't mind drinking out of the same bottle as a Riser."

"I'll risk it," Mabton said. He opened his packet and began to eat the bread and meat, both the characterless but nourishing products of the hydroponics factories. "You know these ducts pretty well," he said around a mouthful of food.

"I memorized the schematic," Ryne said. He paused and added carefully, "After I knew I might have to find my way around."

"Linne is a nice girl," Mabton said cryptically. "Very efficient. We all think a lot of her."

"So do I," Ryne replied.

He waited for Mabton to press the subject. Instead Mabton said, "Can you read the writing on those boxes?"

Ryne glanced at the metallic boxes lining the Core wall. Starting to the left of where he sat, they continued along the curve of the Core and passed out of sight. Each had two sets of symbols on its faceplate. The upper set was in the ancient script. They had been overpainted a long time ago, but their deep intaglio still preserved their outlines legibly. The lower set was in easily readable, standardized print.

" 'Water, heat, atmosphere control . . .' " Ryne read. The remainder were beyond his range of vision. "Shutoffs for the various utilities coming up through the Core," he suggested.

Mabton said, "Did you read from the old script or the modern print?"

It was an unexpected question, and one Ryne wasn't sure he could answer. He said thoughtfully, honestly, "I don't know. I can remember the sounds the old symbols stand for, but with the translations right there, I'm not sure I read the old words."

Mabton stood up. "Fair enough," he said. "Where to now?"

Again the abrupt shift of subject jerked at Ryne. But with a shrug, he put the synkaf flask back in the tool kit and got to his feet. "Back into the Core and then across the cross-section platform to a communication side duct. We follow that until it goes into the main branch. After we've picked up all the side ducts, we start looking for the jam."

He added, "We could save time if you show me where it is."

"How would a simple tech like me know that?" Mabton asked.

Ryne led the way silently back into the Core. Once inside, Mabton grunted, stepped ahead, and quickly led the way across the platform and into the side duct. They followed it to the main branch duct and continued up that to the point where it narrowed to permit the many cables that had now fused into one to pass into the Core again. He stopped, turned on the big lamp, and let its light shine on the cable.

"Just reach out and burn that little bulge you see," he said. "That will take care of it."

Ryne took a torch from his tool kit, adjusted the cutting flame to a thin line, leaned out while still holding to the ladder rung with one hand, and cut away the bulge. A wire flopped free and disappeared into darkness. Taking a can of insulator, he sprayed the raw wound of the cable and then started back down the ladder.

When they reached horizontal again, Mabton said, "Why don't you follow the jam wires back to their source? Then you could play hero for the Coordinator."

"I wasn't told to play spy," Ryne answered thinly. "My job was to break the jam. I assume that's done."

Mabton grinned at him and moved on. At the second side duct, he turned, and now Ryne found the going more difficult. His heavy shoulders kept brushing the sides, and he had to walk bent over. He was relieved when Mabton stopped, opened a door, and led them into the near darkness of a great, empty room.

"The original hydroponics warehouse," Mabton said. "We're under present Lower City now, in the first City— the one they built on top of when they made the three levels."

"Is this the place?"

"Yes," Mabton said. "This is the place." He cocked his head, listening. "They should be here any minute—if some spy didn't find out what we're doing and tell the Coordinator so he could set a trap."

Ryne said quietly, "If you believe that, take off your power pack. You can't fight with it on."

They stood in the near darkness and waited, listening.

II

When they came, it was almost anticlimax. There were two of them, and they walked out of the darkness with torches flicking on to show their features. As soon as Ryne heard Mabton's soft sigh of relief, he knew that these were the people he had been waiting for.

The woman came forward first. Ryne had only brief glimpses of her this night, but he would never forget what she looked like. She was beautiful with the cold beauty of the patrician. Her nose was fine and straight, her eyes large and deep-gray, her hair gold, a color rare in Lower and Upper Cities. For all the firm cast to her mouth there was a sensuality about it that caught Ryne's attention. And when she spoke, the same sensuality was in her husky voice. He also recognized the distinctive accent that marked a High.

She held out a slim hand. "I'm Tara. You must be Ryne."

He nodded and turned as the man came forward. Ryne studied the graying hair, the square face, slightly lined but strong, with the skin strangely roughened. He met Ryne's frank appraisal without expression.

Ryne said suddenly, "Weir! Weir, by all that's holy!"

"Ah, you remember," the man said, "That's pretty good since you haven't seen me in seventeen years."

"You were always in the front row of Listeners when my grandfather read," Ryne said slowly.

He could see the room hollowed out beneath the old family building. He could remember the rows of Listeners sitting on the cold floor as his grandfather's voice rose and

14

fell in the cadences of the old speech. Of all those in the room, only Ryne's grandfather and father understood all the words. Ryne himself could catch a good many; but to the Listeners they were only magnificent sounds. And then Ryne's grandfather would close the Book and translate from memory, using his beautifully modulated voice the way other men used musical instruments. And the group, who had risked their lives coming there, sat quietly, their emotions reflected only in their faces.

Ryne said, "They—my mother told me you died alongside my father fighting the raiders."

"Not so far as I recall," Weir said dryly. "After I pulled you and your grandfather out from under that mob of Bully Boys, I did go back to help your father. He was standing in the escape hatch, holding off fifty Bully Boys while the other Listeners got their women and kids away.

"I tried to help but they clubbed him to death. They split my skull too and left me lying there."

Ryn said, "No one ever seemed to know how the Bully Boys knew where to find us or why they came that night."

"Does it matter now?" Weir asked in his quiet way.

"It matters to me," Ryne said. "One of the reasons I let my mother push me into being a Riser was because I was afraid I'd kill some of the Bully Boys when I got big enough."

"The way you fought seventeen years ago, you had the violence of your father in you," Weir agreed. "Yet we all felt there was enough of your grandfather's gentleness to make you as good a Reader as any."

The way he let his words break off sharpened Ryne's attention. Then Weir said, "You are the Reader, Ryne. When the shock of that raid killed your grandfather, it left only you. There's no other Ryne on this planet. There's no one else who can read so much as a word of the old tongue.

"There are still followers of the Book. We've been waiting for you."

Ryne had not expected this. He had not given his small knowledge of the old tongue a thought these past years. Now he understood the meaning behind Mabton's odd question about the writing on the control boxes circling the Core wall.

"I don't recall much of the language," he said. "I was only ten when my grandfather died. He'd taught me elementary reading and we could talk together in a simple way. But in the four years before I rose, my mother refused to let me use a word of the old speech. She put the blame for everything that happened on the Book and the language it was written in." He added wryly, "I was glad when she finally managed to get me taken as a Riser. It got me away from her."

"She?" Weir echoed. "It wasn't your mother who gave you that chance, Ryne. It was the Coordinator." He shook his head at Ryne's open disbelief. "What would you have done if you'd been responsible for keeping Lower City functioning to provide the labor that fed and clothed and housed the Uppers and Highs—and if there was a potential focal point for trouble in a fourteen-year-old boy?"

He shifted his position. "The Coordinator was new at the job then, and one of his first acts was to have his agents check Lower City. They told him that a lot of the dissidents were waiting for the new Reader to grow up." He grinned sourly. "All of those dissidents supposedly living in the tunnels of the original City, of course, hiding and starving—and waiting."

Mabton spoke suddenly. "That's true, Ryne. The Coordinator made a Riser of you. He bought you with guaranteed security and a full belly."

Ryne swung savagely on him. "If you were bigger, I'd knock you down for that."

Mabton's smile mocked him. "I haven't heard you say anything yet that means much."

Weir moved between them. "Ease up," he said. "Ryne hasn't had a chance to agree or disagree. He doesn't know what we really want of him."

"Didn't Linne tell him?" Mabton asked in surprise.

Ryne looked past Weir at the small man. "Linne told me that you wanted my help, and asked if I'd be willing to listen. She told me there were dozens of exiles and sympathizers, all with one goal—to give the Lowers a chance to live as human beings again. She didn't tell me what you'd want me to do."

"Weir told you," Mabton said stubbornly. "You're the only man who can read the old language."

Weir waved him to silence. "We want you to work with Laszlo," he said. "He's our leader—one of the exiles. He has a plan to build a new City, a one-level City. You're the only man who can help us achieve that plan."

"Another rebellion?" Ryne demanded. "Didn't the riots of a century ago teach anyone anything? You can't destroy this City. The end results would be the same as before—more restrictions, more oppression."

Tara spoke from the shadows behind Weir. "A new City in a new place, Ryne. A City for the Lowers. The Uppers and Highs would remain here. This will be their City, and they'll have to do the work to keep it running."

Weir said, "Laszlo has one of the books from the original ship that brought the first colonists here. We can't read it, but from the pictures we know that it tells how to use the machine that built the first City—and the present City on top of it."

"Does it tell how to build a machine like that?" Ryne asked.

"The original machine still exists," Weir said. "When the time comes, we can get it. And if we can get that book translated, we can make it work for us."

The meaning of his words suddenly struck Ryne, shaking him as his mind filled with a picture of a possible future. Then his shoulders sagged. "I learned so little of the old language. I read children's books, not technical treatises! I . . ."

Weir said quietly, "We aren't here to try to force you to help us. You can go back to Upper City and live out your life the way the Coordinator planned it for you. You'll never get fat, but you'll never know want, either."

Ryne said angrily, "I've waited months since Linne first told me about you. Waited and wondered. I may have buried my memories of what life was like in Lower City, but I've never forgotten them. Don't make me sound like I'm afraid of giving up what I have now!"

He stepped back and glared from one to the other. "I just don't know if I can do what you want me to do. If you want the truth, I'm afraid of failing."

"It's the one chance we have," Weir said. "We ask only an honest effort."

"No," Tara said, "we're asking him to risk everything he has and to take on the responsibility of giving ten thousand people a new life, a new world."

Ryne said simply, "Do I go with you now?"

"No," Weir said. "You don't come with us until the Coordinator sends you into exile."

The remark struck Ryne's sardonic sense of humor. "Good! I'll report back to him and tell him I botched the job and will he please exile me."

"Nothing so crude," Weir said seriously. He jerked his head. "Come along. We have some talking to do."

Tara led the way to a far corner of the room where a once glass-walled cubicle was built against the wall. Here were four chairs and a rickety table. A jug and four mugs sat on the table. When Tara poured a steaming liquid into the mugs and handed them around, Ryne knew that he had been accepted.

"You see," she said, throwing Ryne a light smile, "we were prepared. This is what we call 'tea,' because it's made from leaves like the tea leaves grown on ancient Earth. It's stimulating."

"Especially to the brain," Weir said. "And we need some stimulation right now." He sipped his tea. "We need a plan to have you exiled without arousing the Coordinator's suspicion."

Ryne tried the tea. The taste was faintly bitter and astringent, with a stronger flavor than any he had known before. But after a few sips he found himself liking it and liking the gentle relaxation it spread through his still-taut body.

"I can report Ryne," Mabton suggested. "I'm still a trusted Tech assistant. I can say he refused to follow the jam back to its source."

"That's a start," Ryne agreed. "But it isn't enough for the Upper City bureaucratic mind. The first reaction would be suspicion of you."

He paused and thought. "The simplest plan is to tell the Coordinator the truth with a few minor changes."

"Tell him the plan?" Tara demanded.

"Which he probably already knows about," Weir said dryly.

"Not the plan," Ryne said. "I'll tell him that Mabton and I were trapped on our way out by a group of exiles, but that we managed to fight them off. I'll say I overheard enough to realize that they were trying to kidnap me because I know something about the old language. I can even mention some names—yours, Tara's, this Laszlo's."

"All in the Coordinator's files," Weir said. "But you're too subtle for me, Ryne. All you'll be doing is giving the Coordinator reason to infiltrate us with an agent. He's tried that before. One of these days, he's liable to succeed."

"I expect him to do just that," Ryne said. "And I'll be that agent. If I'm right, the Coordinator will exile me, but as a cover-up. He has my full file, remember, and I'm sure it shows me as the perfectly integrated Riser. He'll think he can trust me. He'll try to use me against you."

"His mind works like Laszlo's," Weir said. "I can see the idea start working inside him and I can see the result— but I'm damned if I can figure what process went on between the beginning and the end."

"Ryne is right," Tara said. "If the Coordinator believes his story, he'll do exactly what Ryne said."

"And if he doesn't believe?" Mabton asked.

"The worst that's happened to anyone the past twenty years has been exile. I'll be with you anyway," Ryne said.

"The Coordinator has the power to rescind the ban on execution," Weir warned him.

"That's the risk I take," Ryne said. He finished his tea. "Mabton and I have been gone long enough." He started out and turned in the doorway. "The Coordinator won't believe a slipshod story. If we managed to fight our way free of a gang of exiles, we'll have to show the proof." He nodded to Weir. "Can you mark us enough to make it look real?"

"If I have to," Weir said. If he noticed that Ryne had quietly taken over the leadership, he gave no indication. Telling Tara to wait, he followed Mabton and Ryne back into the ducts.

They dropped their equipment where the main branch entered the Core. "We'd hardly bother to carry it after being beaten," Ryne said.

"He thinks things through," Weir said to Mabton.

"Let's hope he keeps on doing it," Mabton said.

In the Core itself, Ryne stopped just before it made its final turn to rise vertically. "There's a door just behind us. It leads into a Core guard room. With luck, we can get the Wardens there to call the Coordinator before they finish messing us up."

Weir said, "Just yell 'Coordinator' when you get the door open. I'll leave you that much breath." He swung around suddenly and hit Mabton just below the eye, twisting his knuckles so that the flesh was laid open down Mabton's cheek. Mabton staggered back, hit his head against the wall, and fell to the floor. Weir kicked him a few times without violence.

"I wish you'd taken me first," Ryne said. "I'll fight back whether I want to or not."

"I didn't think about that," Weir said. "I was worrying about hitting Mabton too hard." He scratched his chin. "Maybe I should have done it differently."

With surprising speed and grace, he moved to one side and came at Ryne. "Like this," he added, and hit Ryne twice in the face.

Ryne swung around, raising both hands to a defensive position. Weir brushed them aside and hit him on the mouth, drawing blood. Ryne could feel anger rise, blinding him. He jumped forward, swinging. Weir stepped agilely aside and thumped him in the chest and stomach, and again in the face.

"That should do it," Weir said.

Ryne stopped in midstride and forced himself to relax. Weir said, "Give me time to get out of the Core. And good luck."

Ryne leaned against the wall, breathing deeply. He counted slowly to twenty. Then he shoulder-carried Mabton to the door and pushed it open. The light from the guard room half blinded him. A Warden's club caught him alongside the temple, at the edge of his lamp helmet, before he could see anyone coming.

Mabton fell from Ryne's grasp. Ryne ducked down as he saw movement on the other side. "Call the Coordinator. I'm the scan technician. We . . ."

A club hit him behind the knees. He pitched forward. Another club caught him across the back of the neck. He fell on top of Mabton's limp body and lay breathing gustily.

III

The Wardens must have listened finally, Ryne thought muzzily. He could feel softness beneath him and he could smell the odor of the Accident Ward. He opened his eyes to see Linne looking down at him.

"I'm sorry, Ryne," she said softly.

He misunderstood. "It was the Wardens, the damn Wardens with their clubs."

She looked around as if to make sure there was no one close enough to overhear. "I know. They're being disciplined." She reached down and touched him where his bare hand rested outside the coverlet. "You'll be all right soon. The nurse told me so."

Something was bothering Ryne. He finally brought it to focus in his mind. "The scans—are they working again?"

She laughed shakily. "Of course! They've been working since before you came back. That was two periods ago."

Two periods! Two workshifts, two sleepshifts, two leisureshifts—one-fourth of an entire cycle gone. Ryne cursed the Wardens. He felt cheated, as if he had lost a piece of something precious.

Time was measured in cycles in the City. Each cycle was made up of eight days, with each day containing the three separate shifts. Fifty cycles made up a year. A technician's work pattern was three workshifts on, rest one, two on, rest two in any given cycle. Twice yearly he was allowed a full rest cycle, a full eight-day period attached to the end of the most recent two free days. But the policy was to take a man's sick time from his full rest cycles. The Wardens had cheated him of part of that.

As so often, Linne seemed to know what he was thinking. "Maybe they won't take these days away from you."

Ryne grinned suddenly at his own foolishness. He lifted a hand, beckoning her close to him. His lips against her ear, he said, "If everything works out, it won't matter. I won't be counting time the same way."

Her answer was barely audible. "I didn't know what happened. When do you—go?"

"That's up to the Coordinator."

She laughed, straightening up. "I think you'll be fine soon." Then a brief cloud touched her features. "By the way, you're to report personally to the Coordinator as soon as you're able."

Personally meant in the Coordinator's office, in his actual presence. The interview followed Ryne's first full workshift after his release from the Accident Ward. He stood in front of the polished desk, not sure how to handle himself. He chose a posture of half-attention. He was nodded quickly to a chair.

The Coordinator looked much as he had on the video screen, though in life he seemed taller. He said in his mellifluous voice, "I read the report you dictated. Now that your head is clearer, have you any idea why this gang—I think that's the word you used—tried to kidnap you?"

Ryne had rehearsed this so much he was afraid he wouldn't sound spontaneous. He said, "I can remember a little more now, but I'm still not clear what they wanted. I'm sure one of them said, 'Be careful with him. Laszlo wants him alive to read a book.' "

"Laszlo! I'm not surprised. Did you hear any other names mentioned?"

"Someone called out, 'Keep back. Don't get in the way.' " He stopped briefly. "I can't recall the name, but it sounded like a woman's."

"Ah. Tara, perhaps?"

"That could be it."

The Coordinator nodded. "We can talk about this more when you're fully recovered. Now tell me about the jam."

Ryne described in detail what he had done. The Coordinator said, "According to this Mabton, he suggested you try to trace the wires back to their source. You refused."

"I wasn't ordered to do Warden's work," Ryne said thinly. "I did what I was told."

The Coordinator seemed unperturbed. "We can discuss that later too. For the present, continue working as you have been."

Ryne rose and started for the doorway. The Coordinator called him back. "One more thing. You can expect a bonus for your work and recompense for what happened to you. There'll be enough for a pair-up for you and this girl Linne. If you apply, I'll approve it for a full rest cycle and see that yours and hers are adjusted to match each other."

"Thank you," Ryne said. He left, not knowing whether to be pleased or apprehensive. The Coordinator hadn't reacted quite as he'd hoped. Yet he seemed to have accepted the story, though he had shown little interest in the details. Perhaps at the next session he would ask more questions.

Ryne called Linne as soon as he could, arranging to meet her at the Gardens, the place they went to most.

By the time Ryne dropped three levels, Linne had time to come up two, and so they met at the lifts. She showed her pleasure at the unexpected extra few minutes together. They walked hand in hand along the lighted streets, past shop display windows, and on to the Park area provided for Uppers with their job status. It was a fair-sized expanse of artificial grass and trees and bushes centered by a small pond. At one corner was a playfield for children; at the far rear was a woods, the thick stand of trees and bushes kept comfortably dim for those who wanted a few moments of privacy.

The restaurant was placed so that its terrace overlooked the pond. Ryne seated Linne and brought food from the dispenser. They ate silently but slowly, glancing up now and then to smile at each other.

They had met just a little over a year ago when Linne had been transferred to night-shift communications supervisor. The attraction had been strong and immediate, and both had come to treasure every hour they found to share together. The feeling had continued for Ryne even after Linne confessed that meeting him had been deliberate on her part; that originally she had managed her transfer solely for that purpose; that, in fact, she had become a Riser in part to contact him and influence him to return to those ideals his father and grandfather had preached.

Finished eating, they left the scattering of other diners and walked past the pond toward the dark side of the park. Once they were alone, Linne said, "Can you tell me about it?"

"You haven't heard from them?"

"No, it would be too risky to contact me at a time like this. I'm sure that anyone connected with you is monitored." She glanced at him with a faint smile. "Not that all Risers aren't monitored off and on as a matter of policy."

He told her succinctly what had happened. She said softly, "Do you regret the decision, Ryne?"

He held back his answer until they had slipped through a tunnel of bushes to the tiny hidden clearing where they would be free from observation by other strolling couples. It was a place they had found shortly after their first meeting; and it was, Linne had once told Ryne, one of the few things she liked about Upper City.

They lay side by side, her head lightly on his shoulder. Ryne said, "What is there to regret? Since you first told me why you'd come to Upper City, I've had to face the problem of what my existence means to me. I came to a decision months ago." He thought a moment, "As I told Weir and the others, the only hesitation I had was from fear of not being able to do what they wanted me to do."

She stroked his cheek with soft fingertips. "I think I know you pretty well by now. If it's possible, you'll do it."

He rolled his head and kissed her. They were silent for a few moments. Then he said, "If the Coordinator falls in with my plan, we won't have many more times here."

"Not here, but if Laszlo succeeds, there'll be a lifetime." She hesitated and said almost shyly, "And then there's our full rest cycle just a few shifts away."

"Do you want me to ask for the pair-up license?"

"Yes," she said. "Oh, yes."

When they parted at the entrance to her sleeping quarters, Linne said, "The Coordinator is no fool, Ryne. Don't let wishful thinking make you believe he is one."

He kissed her openly, although there were strolling couples on the street. "For some reason, he frightens me. That's enough to keep me alert."

The full rest cycle was less than one workshift away when Ryne was called to the top level for the second time. This time the Coordinator not only asked him to sit down but personally served him a cup of synkaf.

Ryne took it a bit awkwardly. The Coordinator smiled. "Does my serving you seem so surprising?" He laughed aloud. "It's an old habit, and they're the hardest kind to break."

"Habit?"

"I was once a waiter in the High," the Coordinator said. He explained the meaning of the term 'waiter.' "As you probably know, an Upper can't rise to the High the way a Lower can rise to Upper status." He went on to explain that Uppers, if endowed with certain skills, useful to the Highs, could be taken above when young and apprenticed—as servants—until they proved themselves. Then they were trained to strengthen whatever native skills they possessed. The Coordinator had shown a flair for administration; when he was finished with his training he had been returned to Upper City to work his way up to his present position.

"If all goes well under my administration, my reward will be retirement to the High. My children will become Highs. It is a great honor, a great goal to work for."

He shrugged. "But I didn't bring you here to discuss my past or my future."

"I assumed there was another reason," Ryne said in his dry way.

The Coordinator continued to smile. "Two reasons. First, to tell you that your pair-up license has been approved. You've been assigned a very nice apartment—one with a separate room for the food dispenser."

Ryne sipped his synkaf. He waited for the Coordinator to continue. He said, "Obviously I'm trying to impress you. I want you to have a little taste of what life in the upper echelons of Upper City can be like—and it's much better than anything you might imagine—roomy quarters with separate bedrooms, a license for a child, better-quality foods and wines, more leisure."

"I'm a Riser," Ryne said. "If I ever had any ambitions like that, I stifled them."

"Don't," the Coordinator said. "You're a good technician. You're more than that—you think, you anticipate. You're the kind of man who makes a good Tech Administrator, a Second-Level Upper, with a chance to go a notch higher."

Ryne felt fear stirring inside, and excitement. He wondered if the Coordinator was going to fall in with the plan.

He said, "Why me?"

"Because something needs repairing—and you're the only technician who can do it," the Coordinator said.

"Repairing? What?"

"The City," the Coordinator said. "It's like a giant machine—no, that's not a good analogy."

He leaned toward Ryne, his expression intense. "Did you ever do much thinking about the City, Ryne? I mean the whole—from the top to the bottom. The entire living, breathing organism that exists under what we call the Dome?"

Ryne shook his head. The City? It was there. It was something he and everyone else he knew accepted.

"Did you ever wonder where it came from? Why it was built? What it really is?"

Ryne thought. He's trying to trap me into admitting I know more than the schools taught Lowers. Then he wondered what difference that would make. The Coordinator must know who his father and grandfather had been, the environment that had influenced him as a child.

He said, "When our ancestors came to this world, one group wanted to try to live in the open as Earth people had. The other wanted to be protected as they had been in the ship that brought them here. It was this group that built the City. The others struggled for a time against the terrible weather of the Out and against the wild animals. Then they disappeared, but we don't know whether they died or moved to a better part of the planet."

"You're close enough," the Coordinator said. "Go on."

Ryne said, "The original City was on one level, but as time passed two social groups developed—those who labored and those who managed. They lived side by side until the Highs came from space. They had a higher technology and they used it to gain control of the City. When they had complete control, they took the machine that had built the original City and made it build a new City on top of the old, a City with three levels instead of one. The Highs put the workers on the lowest level, the managers above them, and themselves at the top. By giving privileges to those just below them—the Uppers—the Highs kept their loyalty."

"That sounds like a lesson you learned from your grandfather," the Coordinator said. "I'm not going to waste time arguing the truth of it or the logic of our system. It's enough for you to remember that whatever you once were, now you're an Upper."

He moved closer to Ryne. "And as an Upper, you—and any child you may have—own a share in the City. You're part of it. Think of the City as an organism, the term I used a moment ago. It lives to protect us, to sustain us. It keeps away the terrors and dangers and discomforts of the Out, and it feeds and clothes us. It provides the air we breathe, the water we require, the food we need. It is never too warm nor too cold. It takes little from us physically because our bodies never need to adjust to changes in climate."

He saw that he was stepping beyond the limits of Ryne's understanding. "Climate—changes in weather. Something none of us have ever known except through the old films that show Earth and the planets our ancestors colonized in the early days of space exploration.

"Imagine if you can, Ryne, a world where food depends on the whims of a hostile nature. If there isn't enough rainfall—water from the sky—or if there's too much wind or if too many wild things want to eat the food man grows from the soil, if any one of these things should happen men starve. If men are caught in the open—the Outs of their worlds—without proper clothing or shelter, they die from too much heat or cold. And there are tiny living things called viruses and microbes which invade such men's bodies and cause terrible sickness or death. Ryne, many men who have no cities such as ours have died in great pain from weather or disease or wild animals attacking them."

The Coordinator took a breath. "We're protected from all of these things. But what we get, we have to pay for. And each of us pays according to his ability. That's an ancient truism, but one as right today as when it was first said."

He leaned forward suddenly. "What do you picture when you think of the High?"

Ryne had never seen so much as a video projection of a High, but he had been told a great deal as a child and in school. He said, "As people. Very clever people who work very hard to keep the City working for us all."

The Coordinator's lips drew back in a semblance of a smile. He turned away quickly, standing up and striding now as he talked. "The entire City is one organism. It's like a man. The head, the brain—this is the High. It's the nerve center that guards the rest of the body and instructs it. The heart that pumps the blood up and down to nourish the organism—this is Upper City. All the other working parts of the body are Lower City. Here are the great lungs that pump lifegiving air, the organs that strain out the poisons. Here are the parts that do the physical work—the arms and legs, the muscles—to create energy, food.

"All of these are of equal importance to the organism, to the City. No man can live without a brain or a heart or lungs. And if one part is badly injured, the other parts suffer. Destroy one and the whole organism is destroyed."

He spoke eloquently. His words, his phrasing, his expression all held Ryne in rigid silence. He leaned forward, concentrating so he wouldn't miss any of the word picture being painted, any of the ideas the Coordinator's resonant voice was bringing to him. When the voice died away, Ryne leaned back. He was tired, and his hand shook a little as he lifted his cup.

The Coordinator was waiting for him to speak. He said finally, "But why me? What can I do?"

He spoke almost without conscious thought of the role he had come here to play. The Coordinator's spell was on him and the next words appeared to weave the mesh more thickly.

"I want you to be the doctor. To cure the disease that threatens the organism—the City." He stepped forward.

"One of its vital parts is threatened, Ryne—Lower City. If you fail, it will wither and cease to function. And then the entire City will die.

"And we'll die too—you and I and your Linne. Highs, Uppers, Lowers. And any hope of civilization on this world."

IV

The Coordinator stopped and took a brief turn about the room. "Think about it that way," he said. He was silent, leaving Ryne alone for the moment.

Ryne thought about it, and he realized the Coordinator had made a mistake. The man had frightened him before; his mind was quick and trained more than Ryne's could ever hope to be. But by pausing, he had broken the spell of his words, and Ryne was able to lift the net that had been settling around him.

"I don't understand what I can do," he repeated.

The Coordinator sat facing him. "I'll be frank with you, Ryne. I have agents throughout Lower City—for the protection of everyone, not to harass. They aren't always successful in getting information, but they do hear things—words not meant for their ears, rumors. All of these I synthesize. When I see a thread persisting, I try to track it down. What I'm going to tell you now is one of those threads.

"Laszlo has found some of the old books in the ancient script, books from the original ship. And he found something in those books that can be a threat to our existence."

"Do you mean information about weapons?" Ryne asked.

If the Coordinator knew that Ryne was acting he gave no sign. He said, "I don't know. That's one of the things I need to find out. But I do know that only one man in the City—perhaps on this entire world—could possibly translate the ancient script into language meaningful to Laszlo. That man is you."

Ryne was on firm ground now. He knew what to say to the Coordinator. "I learned so little in the first place, and I've forgotten most of that."

"Not forgotten, only pushed to the back of your mind," the Coordinator said. He smiled thinly at Ryne. "I have complete files on the history of the Readers and Listeners. I know how each succeeding Reader was groomed by his predecessor. I know that from the time you first began to talk, you were subjected to both our language and the ancient one. Before you learned to read in school, you were reading simple children's books in the ancient language. The knowledge is still in you, Ryne."

He nodded as if answering a question Ryne had been about to ask. "That's why you're the one man who can help. I want to give you to Laszlo and his group. I want you to find out what you're expected to read—and what it means. And then I want you to report that information to me. I want you to learn every detail of Laszlo's plan to destroy us; I want to know those details. In no other way can I be in a position to heal the wounds he'll inflict on the City."

The analogy had fascinated, hypnotized, Ryne before. Now its magic was gone. He said in a puzzled tone, "I can't just go down and ask Laszlo to take me in—not after the way I fought to get away."

"No," the Coordinator agreed. "But you can get them to help you in such a way that you'll logically be grateful to them for doing so. You can go down as an Exile."

The victory was almost too easy; and suddenly Ryne was afraid. He was not just afraid that the Coordinator was playing with him, but afraid of the very word itself. Exile!

He had seen an Exile briefly when he was a boy. A youngish man who had risen (some years before) was sent back on suspicion of being an activist against Upper City. He came back to Lower City with nothing but the rough jumper worksuit of a Lower, the pockets empty. Bully Boys were waiting for him, and only quick intervention by friends saved him from being beaten to death. But once he was healed of his beating, he still had nothing. There was no work for him, and a man in Lower City without work was a man without access to food or shelter. His friends helped as much as their limited means allowed. But he soon disappeared. Ryne recalled the rumors—he had died of starvation; he had killed himself; he had been caught and turned into the Out, to be devoured by the wild animals there or to die of the terrible summer heat or winter cold. Then Ryne remembered his name. It had been Corso.

The Coordinator said, "You'll have to fight when you first go into Lower City. But Laszlo's people should be there, waiting to help you. I'll make sure that they know you're being exiled. They'll save you so they can use you."

"But what if I can't learn enough of the old tongue to be of use?" Ryne demanded. "What happens to me then?"

Instead of answering, the Coordinator asked, "Do you remember your grandfather reading? Do you remember the Listeners when he read first in the ancient tongue and then translated?"

"I remember people laughing sometimes—not because anything was funny but from pure pleasure and excitement. And I remember some of them crying. Now and then someone would cry, 'Yes! Yes!' "

"Did you ever read from the Book?"

"Only to Grandfather. I was just beginning to learn it when the raid happened."

"But you remember what the Book said?"

Not clearly, Ryne had to admit. It had been too long ago; he had been too young. He tried to put into words what little he could recall. "It was about the things great men of the past—men of Earth—had thought and written for others. It was about the way of life on Earth before men were driven to seek living room on other worlds. It wasn't exciting like a story. A lot of the words didn't mean too much to me, in either language."

The Coordinator nodded. "That's good enough. I think you can do it, Ryne. Are you willing? I'm not asking an easy thing of you. It could be very dangerous. If your true reason for being there is ever suspected . . ."

He paused there, leaving the remainder of what he might have said to Ryne's imagination. Ryne sat silently, his expression thoughtful. He said finally, "And after it's over—if I succeed—what happens to me, to Linne?"

"If you succeed, you'll be promoted with a chance to work up to Second Level." He waved away Ryne's next question. "The Exile will not be a permanent part of your record. That's merely a device to make you look genuine. You'll be accused, tried, and sentenced. But once you've been taken by Laszlo's group, that record will be completely destroyed."

"And if I fail?" Ryne persisted.

"If you've made an honest effort, nothing will have changed," the Coordinator said. "You return to things as they are. Perhaps you'll be given a one-notch promotion; you won't be penalized."

He went to his desk and returned with two large holophotos. One was of a man. The Coordinator said, "Laszlo." Ryne studied the lean, bony face. The olive skin stretched taut across high cheekbones. The mouth was thin, the nose long and deeply indented at the bridge. But the dark eyes caught Ryne's attention. They burned from the picture as if peering into his brain. Through them he could feel the intensity of the man, the dedication. His father had had much that same dedication, but in him there had been a compassion. In Laszlo, Ryne could sense none.

"He was born an Upper," the Coordinator said. "His brilliance caught the interest of the Highs early and he was taken up and trained to be a research scientist. He was regarded very favorably to the point where he was allowed a close friendship with a High official's daughter. Then he was discovered in the act of sabotaging the laboratory where he worked. He was destroying all the records and substituting others that would make it appear as if the High were trying to create semi-robots of the Lowers, to turn them into perfect servants. Writings were found in his quarters—writings that showed clearly he intended to tear down the structure of the City and to rebuild it according to his own ideas of what was right.

"He was exiled to Lower City. There he immediately disappeared. That was a year and a half ago."

Ryne said skeptically, "How do you know he's still alive?"

"Rumors," the Coordinator said promptly. "And who else would have conceived that plan to jam the scans at a time when you would have to be the man to go and fix the jam? He did it not to annoy us but to capture you, Ryne. All the information I've been able to get points directly to that."

He handed Ryne the other picture. It was of the incredibly aristocratic and beautiful woman he had met so briefly. "That's Tara," the Coordinator said. "She was the daughter of the High official I mentioned. She worked as Laszlo's assistant, and when he was exiled, she was also suspected of sabotage. She was sent here for rehabilitation. But it was a waste of time. Finally she too had to be exiled to Lower City; and from there, like Laszlo, she disappeared. Together they make a dangerous team."

He took back the photographs. "The last day of your rest cycle—of your pair-up with your Linne—you'll be arrested. But until then, there will be no trouble. So enjoy yourself." He smiled faintly. "But don't forget to continue your daily work at the gymnasium. You may need all the strength and skill you have when you reach Lower City. The Bully Boys will be waiting."

"And you won't tell the Wardens to keep them off me?" Ryne demanded.

"If I do, Laszlo will be suspicious," the Coordinator said. "We just have to risk it. They should rescue you before you're too badly hurt. Besides, a man of your size and in your physical condition should be able to handle quite a few Bully Boys." He added, as if the thought pleased him, "If you break a few of their heads, no one will really object."

Ryne took a deep breath and stood up. "I'll do my best," he said, and started for the door.

He stopped and looked back questioningly. "Linne?"

"Don't concern yourself," the Coordinator said promptly. "Once you've been accepted by Laszlo, I'll bring her here and make sure she understands the situation. You don't have to worry that you'll come back and find you've lost her to someone else."

"Thank you," Ryne said. He left. As the lift carried him down to his level, he wondered how long it would be before he came up here again. And he realized suddenly that he could never return unless he actually put himself on the Coordinator's side.

The thought was briefly, fleetingly tempting. The life of a Second-Level Upper was a good one—it meant comfort beyond anything he had ever hoped for; it meant security; it meant status for his child.

And it meant that for every Upper who enjoyed those things, a dozen Lowers lived in hopeless hungry emptiness from their birth to relief in death.

He smiled thinly, thinking of Linne's remark that he was very suggestible. For a brief few moments back there he had been caught in the net of the man's eloquence. But now he was free.

He laughed aloud. Free? Free to follow the dictates of a man like Laszlo. Free to risk his life for Lowers, many of whom cared for nothing more than what they had, and who would resent anything anyone might try to do for them.

But it wasn't those people he was working for, Ryne realized suddenly. It was their children and their children's children.

He went on down, relieved and at the same time unsure of himself.

V

A full rest cycle could be a terribly short time, Ryne discovered, but it was long enough for him to learn things about Linne he had not known before. He found that two people could live in joy and sorrow at the same time. There was joy at their being together; and there was sorrow for what lay so soon ahead—with the growing possibility that this could well be their last time together.

With each day, the uneasy conviction grew in both of them that the Coordinator's quick decision to exile Ryne had more behind it than luck for Laszlo's cause. When Ryne would go off to the gymnasium for his prescribed exercise, Linne would "shop"; and then they would lie close together, whispering in case a sounding device had been planted in their almost too elegant quarters.

On the last day they were together, Ryne summed up for them both. "The kind of defensive and offensive tactics they teach me looked helpful at first. And they would be against one or two or even three Bully Boys. But they contain the kind of violence that would only make a mob angry and leave me open to attack."

He was whispering with his lips close to her ear. He ran a hand over her soft hair. "And the information you picked up—wherever you get it—sounds no better." He was referring to a recent tightening of security regulations in Lower City, a new review of the files of all Risers, an increase in the number of Auxiliaries, those semi-trained forces of Uppers under the Coordinator's command, and the rumored creation of a new network of paid Lower agents—their rewards in the form of food and those small but eagerly wanted privileges for people to whom any concession was a privilege.

"Do I report this to Weir and the others?"

"They already know," Linne answered. "What we can't find out is where all this is leading. In some ways the Coordinator seems to be anticipating us; in others he seems to be reacting to panic. We just don't know what to expect."

And then suddenly their chance to worry about the problem together was ended. A knock came at the door the last morning. Two men in the uniforms of Auxiliaries waited there. The taller said politely, "You're to come with us. Suspicion of subversion."

Linne played her role well, Ryne thought. "But that's impossible!" she cried. "He's been rewarded for . . ."

Ryne turned and kissed her. "Some administrative mistake," he said. "I'll see you soon."

Her lips under his lifted in a quivering smile. Then she turned away and Ryne went with the two men. He had nothing more than the clothes he was wearing, and once in detention those were taken from him except for his boots. Before midday he found himself in a courtroom, facing a judge and the charge council. He stood before the judge's bar, uncomfortable in the stiff gray jumper suit he had been given. In silence he listened to the charge against him.

One Ryne, nightshift Scan Technician . . .

The formal language seemed to go on endlessly. But in essence he was accused of failing to follow up the scan jam tap because he wanted to protect those responsible. It was a flimsy enough charge and one that would never have stood up in the face of a defense. But the Coordinator had seen to it he was permitted no defense; after all, the temporary written record of the charge and of his sentencing and the word-of-mouth rumors were the important things here.

He heard the heavy word "exile," and within the hour he was on his way down the lift shaft to the Fishbowl, as Lowers called the glass-walled room where the lift stopped. Ryne had entered it as a Riser those many years before. Then he had been treated with a kind of stiff courtesy by the two Wardens who manned the room. Now there was none of that courtesy. He was unceremoniously herded to the doorway leading into Lower City.

Ryne walked expressionlessly forward, forcing himself to look through the heavy glasslike walls at the dim streets stretching outward. He could see a line of people forming, most with dull expressions showing faint flickers of hope that they would find excitement to break the grinding monotony of their lives. The other faces Ryne remembered only too well—the anticipation in the expressions of the Bully Boys spreading themselves quietly through the crowd. They stood out, not only in their youngness but in their strength and energy. Poorly fed by Upper City standards, they were still in better physical condition than other Lowers. The Wardens saw to that.

Ryne opened the door. He took a step forward and stopped, listening to the door click shut behind him. The people had fallen into two lines, forming a gauntlet he would have to run. And at its end would be what? He had no immediate answer. Beyond the end of the street he faced there was nothing but more Lower City, more dreary, stained buildings and dim streets. And everywhere was the stench that he had almost forgotten—the indefinable but all-pervading odor of tired poverty and decay and hopelessness.

Ryne started walking because there was nothing else to do. He had no idea where he could go. If he was to be rescued, he saw no signs of anyone who might offer him help. And he could think of no one who would befriend him, give him food or shelter, if he did get through the growing mob. He kept moving, steadily, not too fast and not too slowly.

He was halfway along the line when a rough young voice called, "How does it smell to you, Riser?"

"His name is Ryne," an old woman's voice said. "I remember him when he was a boy. He was in the Reader's family."

"One of them do-nothings," a young male voice sneered. "One of them smart ones with a lot of talk and no guts to fight."

Ryne turned his head to look into vicious features, hungry for destruction, hungry for some way to satisfy the need for violence that was always part of a Bully Boy.

"He don't look glad to get back!" a woman called jeeringly.

Ryne continued to walk. He could feel movement behind him now and he knew that the line was closing ranks. He never did learn who threw the first piece of crumbling brick. It struck him on the temple, sending a thin trace of blood down his cheek. The line began to close ahead of him now, and he could smell the peculiar stench of mob excitement.

He shook his head, not giving them the satisfaction of wiping away the blood, and pushed on. Now they had a wall formed against him. Another piece of brick struck him on the shoulder, the pain of it making him blink. Faces leered at him, some mocking, some simple, some openly vicious. He tried to curb his anger against the older people, knowing what motivated them. But he made no effort to hide his contempt for the Bully Boys. He swung his heavy shoulders, forcing his way toward the nearest of them.

"Move aside," Ryne said to the older people in his way. His voice was pitched low. "I don't want to hurt any of you real Lowers."

A well-fleshed figure between youth and manhood stepped in front of him. "Who do you want to hurt, Riser?"

Ryne reached out, catching the other by a solid wrist. He applied pressure, twisting the way he had been taught in the gymnasium. Few could see what he was doing, but none could miss the result. The young man screamed in anguish and went to his knees.

Ryne released him. "Move aside!" he repeated.

"We'll knock the Upper out of him for that!" a boy's voice screamed. It came from behind Ryne. He tried to turn, feeling the threat, but the crowd had him too tightly pinned now. He felt the first touch of the brick as it was slammed violently against his skull. Then everyone seemed to melt away, giving him room to fall. He went to his knees and remained that way, his head hanging. A foot came out and caught him alongside the head. Another smashed into his mouth. Someone shouted in glee and came down on his back with the full weight of a standing jump. Ryne collapsed to the dirty pavement. He barely felt the kicks and blows that drummed on him.

Then fingernails raked his forehead, clawing for his eyes, and he completely lost control. With a cry of sheer terror, he reached out both hands and caught two slim wrists. He jerked, rolling over and kicking up with his knee. The woman cried out as she was flung away. He began lashing with his feet and the crowd fell back. Ryne staggered up, blood running from his bruised face, from the corner of his mouth, and from his nostrils. He saw a boy with a rock and he started for him, his face a mask of savagery.

The boy dropped his rock and turned, stumbling as he ran. A foot came out to trip Ryne. He turned, caught a man before he could run, and hit him viciously in the face. The man's weight sagged down on Ryne's hands. He lifted the body and threw it at a group of six moving toward him.

"He's crazy. He'll kill us!" someone shrieked. Half of the crowd scattered as a wave of panic moved over them. The remainder fell back, watching Ryne. He turned to see that there was no one behind him. Sucking in a steadying breath, he began walking up the street again. Small knots of silent watchers fell away as he neared them. The Bully Boys had disappeared, fleeing for the moment into whatever holes they had crawled out of. Ryne forgot them. He forgot everything but the need to keep moving, to get someplace where he might find safety.

He reached the intersection and he was alone. He took one more step and felt himself falling. He sprawled on the street and lay there, knowing he should move before they came back and kicked him again—and knowing that he could not move.

He heard footsteps. Voices that had become familiar in their viciousness brushed his ears. They were coming back; they would kill him this time.

And then he heard a cold, clear voice slashing through the curses and chatters of ecstasy from those moving toward him. "You stinking animals. Get away before we break you into pieces!"

The voices was somehow familiar, but too blurred for Ryne to place. He tried to lift his throbbing head but he could manage only a faint jerking. Hands caught him beneath the armpits and lifted him to his knees. Now he could hear other footsteps, quick, running ones coming toward him.

The voice of the man holding him said, "Carry him easy. He's pretty badly beaten."

Motion nauseated Ryne and he rolled his head to vomit. But the feeling ended quickly as he lost consciousness.

VI

Ryne awoke to the lingering familiarity of the dark, close odors of his childhood, and he knew that he was in a basement room somewhere in Lower City. He tried to lift his eyelids and to raise his head, but the effort was too great and he lay back quietly.

"He's awake," the last voice he remembered hearing said. The voice wasn't as cold now as it had been. A hand touched his shoulder. "Easy, Ryne. You're safe now."

Ryne recognized Mabton's sharp tones. He tried to answer and winced as pain battered at his lips. Another hand, smaller than Mabton's, and more gentle, slid under his back and lifted him slightly. A different voice, a woman's, murmured, "I'm bringing a cup to your mouth. Be careful. It's hot tea."

His lips hurt as the liquid slid over them. But he liked the astringent taste of the tea cleansing his mouth and the warmth of it working through his body. He took three swallows before the cup was taken away. "That's enough for now," the woman said. Fuzzily, Ryne recalled that her name was Tara, and that she was beautiful.

"When can we take him?" Mabton asked.

"He'll have to rest a good while before he can make that trip," Tara answered. "It's only been three days since we brought him here."

Mabton laughed. "Ryne's not soft. He hung right in there when we made the trip along the ducts. And he gave back a lot of that beating he took—with interest. Let his bruises ease up and he can make the trip."

What trip, Ryne wondered. His mind fastened on

Tara's words: " . . . only three days." He had been unconscious that long!

"I say give him a full cycle," Tara said.

A cycle! The idea appalled Ryne. But more than a cycle passed before he could see clearly, before he could sit up and take nourishment without help, and before he could attend to his own needs in the bathroom down the dim, damp hallway.

When he could look around, he found little to see. The room was as drab as it smelled, dismally lighted by one ancient type of lamp bulb hanging from the ceiling, a few pieces of battered furniture, and an old black-clothed crone who tended to his wants until he was able to handle himself. The cycle and more passed before he saw anyone else.

He was sprawled on the bed, feeling pleased at the quickness with which his strength returned after the occasional draining of his energy required by walking down the hall. The door opened to let Tara in. Deep-gray eyes measured him, and then her full, mobile mouth lifted in a smile.

"You look almost human again," she said. "You can leave in a few days."

"Leave for where?"

She gave him a surprised look. "You don't know? You weren't told?" Ryne shook his head, and she gestured toward the half-full mug and empty plate by his bed. "Where do you think your food comes from? Your tea?"

Ryne hadn't thought about it; but then he hadn't really tasted the food either except to notice that the old crone had a knack for scorching everything. He wasn't yet up to thinking about it. He shook his head again.

"The Out," Tara said.

Ryne felt the ice of fear run through him, a totally irrational and uncontrollable fear. The Out! He could hear his mother threatening him with the Out, with the savage beasts and the terrible climate—the summer heat and winter cold and the violent storms that could batter a human body to insensibility within minutes. Ryne's concept of weather and seasons and storms was vague at best, gleaned from old tales and schoolbooks, as was his knowledge of wild beasts. Yet they became vivid horrors in his child's mind.

And after the raid that killed his father and caused his grandfather's death, his mother continued to talk of the Out—of the men who were sent there, the last stage of Exile. Had he ever known of any who came back?

And he recalled sharply being taken as a boy to the strangely wide gates at the far side of Lower City. Now he knew that those gates were set in the City's shell, its opaque wall of force that kept the Out at bay. But then he had thought of them as opening onto the end of the world. His mother had shown him the solidly closed gates and the crisscross of light beams that provided the alarm system.

"If you're really bad, they open that little door in the big gate and send you through—into the Out," she had told him. He had been six years old at the time.

The Out! In a few days he would be going there. Fear was a tangible wave of icy, fetid air about him. He reached for his tea and his hand shook so that he slopped some on the coverlet under him.

"We all live there," Tara said. "It's quite safe."

"If you say you live there, then I have to believe it's safe. My mind has to believe; my emotions can't yet," Ryne said.

"You'll adjust quickly enough," she assured him. "But don't think about it. Exercise your body by walking around here, but let your mind rest some more."

She added, "And I mean stay here—in this room or in the hall. Don't go into the streets."

"The Bully Boys are still looking for me after all this time?"

"And the Wardens," she said. "But especially the Bully Boys. It seems you gave one a little too much of his own medicine. They still aren't sure he'll recover. Just stay off the streets."

"All right," Ryne said.

After she had gone, he thought about her injunction about the Out. With grim humor, he wondered which was the better choice—facing the Bully Boys and Wardens in the streets or facing the Out?

Not that it mattered, of course; he really had no choice at all.

The Coordinator rapped the dispatch on his desk with a stiff finger. "I gave orders for Ryne to be beaten, not half killed. Why didn't the Wardens keep the Bully Boys under better control?"

"I sent the message as you instructed," the Secretary said.

The Coordinator waved him to a chair. "Listen to me carefully so that you'll understand the reason for the instructions I'll give you. I want no hesitation, no questioning. I want immediate action."

"The Secretary sat down. The Coordinator said, "Ryne is the one hope we have of getting information in time to act on it. Until we know the final step to Laszlo's plan, we're helpless."

"The Auxiliaries," the Secretary suggested weakly, "are . . ."

"Dammit, man, why do you think I went to all the trouble of falling in with Laszlo's childish scheme of contacting Ryne and then having him get me to exile him? Because I need Ryne's ability to read the old language as much as Laszlo does."

He frowned at the uncomprehending look on the Secretary's face. "You're aware that—no, of course you aren't, since you're new here." He paused and began again. "You should know that I had Ryne brought up here because as a potential reader he could develop into a threat to us. I also had the girl, Linne, brought up when I learned she was being trained as their chief spy. They think they manipulated her rising; but it was I, not they."

The Secretary shook his head in disbelief. "You say she's an agent, yet you made her a Communications Supervisor?"

"Of course. Think, man, who else is in a better position to transmit to Laszlo the information I want him to have? Whenever I want something passed on, I let this girl, Linne, discover it. She takes care of the difficulties for me. But she's very clever. More than once she's sent out information I didn't want Laszlo to know."

He waved her aside with a brusque movement of his

hand. "But Ryne is the problem. He thinks I've sent him to discover that Laszlo's plan is to build a new City just for Lowers."

One of his rare moments of anger caught him. "A new City for Lowers! Do you realize what that means to us—no one to work the factories, run the utilities. We do the work ourselves or we go hungry, choke for lack of air, live in darkness, die of thirst! I didn't spend my life working to end up as a factory slave!"

The Secretary said, "This machine, can't you have it destroyed?"

"If I knew where it was, yes. But Laszlo hid it after some fool Outer showed it to him. That's one of the things I want Ryne to learn—where the machine is. But that won't be enough. He has to discover the final step in Laszlo's plan, the one thing we have to know. Our chances of destroying the machine are very slim. I'm going on the assumption that ultimately Laszlo will succeed in building his new City. What I must find out is how he plans to get the Lowers from this City to that one!"

The Secretary said fumblingly, "You think that if Ryne manages to translate the Book so that Laszlo can build the City, then Laszlo will have to tell him the final step in the plan—how he's going to get the Lowers from this City."

"That's what I said," the Coordinator snapped. "He has to tell the plan sooner or later. He can't do it by himself."

"But if Ryne isn't really one of us . . ."

"He isn't," the Coordinator said. "His psych-profile showed clearly that his early childhood had a tremendous influence on him. He was a potential focal point for rebellion. I told you that was why I had him brought up. He buried those feelings, yes, but this Linne brought them back to the surface. No, Ryne is their man, not ours."

"Then," the Secretary said with bold stubbornness, "even if Ryne does learn the rest of Laszlo's plan, how can we get the information from him?"

The Coordinator smiled. "As time goes on, Ryne will learn that he can walk in the City with immunity. I'll see to that. Also, he will contact me at regular intervals—either because he thinks he might gain information from me or because Laszlo instructs him to. Then a day will come when Ryne enters the City and finds that he no longer has that immunity. He will be easy to capture. And once I have him again, I can get the information I want."

The Secretary looked shocked. "You can't torture a man . . ."

"Of course not. No more than I could order Laszlo's assassination. It's as much against my conditioning as it is against yours. But I don't need torture to get Ryne to talk. I have something very important to him—something I'll trade for his information. I have his Linne."

The Secretary showed his admiration by his expression. Then he said, "Wouldn't it have been simpler not to have let Ryne go at all? If he doesn't translate the Book, how can Laszlo ever build his new City?"

"Don't be a fool, man. Laszlo is a skilled scientist. Given time, he can figure it out. Oh, it would take him a few years—three or four—but sooner or later, he'd make that machine work."

He rose from the chair in his restless way. "I'm retiring in a few years. Do you think they'll take me into the High, make Highs of my children, if I leave a threat like Laszlo as the legacy for my successor? No, Laszlo's plan must be destroyed once and for all—and destroyed soon. That's why I sent Ryne. He's the only man who can make it happen within a short time."

He sat down again. "Now understand me. Send orders that until further notice, Ryne is not to be molested in any way by anyone whenever he appears in Lower City. That order goes to the Wardens immediately.

"Once I know that Laszlo has finally divulged the last step in his plan—the way he intends to get the mass of Lowers to leave this City—then I'll rescind that order. But until then, it stands!"

"How can the lowers leave whether or not Laszlo wants them to?" the Secretary argued. "We control the gates to the Out. If they should attack, there are the Wardens and the Auxiliaries."

"Laszlo knows that as well as we do," the Coordinator snapped. "Whatever plan he devises will take our strengths into account. That's why I have to know what he intends. He's clever.

I have to be in a position to be a little more clever."

Part of the Secretary's job was to stimulate the Coordinator's thought processes by putting forth arguments and objections to whatever decisions the Coordinator planned. He said now, "What if we do succeed—if we destroy Laszlo's plan and, ultimately, his machine? How will that prevent others from going into the Out and forming the core of another rebel group? There has always been one or another underground since the Highs came."

"True. But remember, until Weir and his friends went into the Out after the raids seventeen years ago, the dissidents lived in the sewers. But Weir knew enough history to realize he could risk the Out. Yet if it hadn't been for the colony of Outers who live nearby, he and his friends would never have survived. No City-bred man could live without help. He would need too long to adapt to the different conditions. If there were no Outers, no group could follow this present one into the Out."

He stabbed a finger at the Secretary. "Once I defeat Laszlo, once I find his machine and have him and his people in custody, then I'll send my Auxiliaries into the Out. With our technology, we'll run that colony of Outers so far away that they can't help any furture dissidents. And before I destroy the machine, I'll use it to build a barrier no man can penetrate. Then I'll have full control. My successor will inherit a stable, peaceful City.

"Now, go send those orders I gave you. And check back. See that they're carried out with no mistakes."

VII

Ryne's restlessness grew as his rate of healing increased. Soon he was able to move about easily, with no signs of weariness. But Tara insisted that he stay awhile longer.

"The trip isn't easy. Neither is meeting Laszlo," she said. "Give yourself a few more days."

Ryne knew his needs well enough to realize that just hiking up and down the gloomy hallway wouldn't build his strength. What he needed was a series of good long walks, even some jogging when he felt up to it. He grinned a little, thinking of Tara's reaction when he told her he'd gone out for a long walk. Then maybe she'd agree to let him leave this semi-prison. He no longer feared going into the Out; reason told him that he could survive if Tara and the others had.

He had to do some maneuvering to escape the watchful eye of the old crone. Finally he caught her dozing and slipped out of the room quietly. He turned to his left, toward the stairs rather than the bathroom down the hall. They twisted upward to what seemed at first to be a solid wall. He felt along it until he found the crack marking the edge of a doorway. A strong push and a panel in the wall swung back, revealing a street-level hall with the outside door only a few meters away.

Ryne hesitated only briefly before opening the door and stepping into the stench of Lower City. What lay in front of him was no more prepossessing than the room he'd left, Ryne thought with sour humor, but it was less confining. At this hour of the afternoon, the street was empty in both directions. An hour or so from now it would be filled with workers as the factory shifts changed, and so Ryne decided to limit himself to no more than thirty minutes. He turned to his right and started up the narrow sidewalk.

Then the street was no longer empty. At the corner ahead, three Bully Boys appeared. They stopped, leaning against a building wall and watching him in silence. He turned to go in the other direction. He glanced back as he passed the doorway he had just come through. Two of the Bully Boys had peeled themselves from the building and were coming slowly toward him. He flexed his hands, wondering if he had the strength to fight.

He moved closer to the doorway and waited for them. They came steadily, swaggering, clearly relishing their self-proclaimed importance. Behind the pair, the third Bully Boy had been joined by three others. That made six, more than he could handle. The first two were close enough now for him to see the anticipation on their faces. Ryne tensed himself. They might get him, but before they did he'd have the satisfaction of wiping the expressions off this pair.

A flicker of movement on the left caught Ryne's attention. A Warden vehicle was coming around the far corner toward him. Two Wardens were visible through the protective transparent bubble covering the passenger compartment. The one beside the driver had his riot club ready, the butt resting on his thigh.

Ryne moved backward, his hand reaching for the door latch. He jerked at it and felt the resistance. He jerked again. The door refused to yield. In front of him the Warden vehicle had reached the curb. The Bully Boys were only a half-dozen strides away, walking faster now. The bubble door swung open and the Warden with the riot club jumped out.

Ryne began pounding his fist against the door panel. A Bully Boy laughed at him. The oncoming Warden grinned and lifted his club so that Ryne could see him adjust the power of the charge it held. Ryne stopped wasting his strength in futile anger and crouched slightly, waiting for the three to reach him.

A sudden sharp keening came from the vehicle. The Warden stopped and turned, looking at his partner. He gave a hand signal and the Warden close to Ryne held out his club, stopping the Bully Boys. The man in the vehicle was using the communicator, frowning as he listened. He hung it back on the dashboard and gave another hand signal. It had no meaning for Ryne but it made the Warden swear angrily.

One of the Bully Boys laughed. "Duties, Warden? Leave Ryne to us. We'll bring you the pieces."

"You'll get the hell away from here—all of you," the Warden snapped.

"Hey, this is that exiled Riser," The Bully Boy said. "He—"

"I said, move!"

They both hesitated briefly and then turned, going slowly back the way they'd come. One turned and called, "Later, Riser. Later."

The Warden nodded at Ryne. His expression was hungry. "Remember that, Ryne." Turning, he stumped back to the vehicle and climbed in. It moved off down the street, following the Bully Boys as if to make sure they kept going. Ryne could see the driver explaining something to his still-angry partner.

Behind Ryne the door came open suddenly. A hand caught his shoulder and jerked him inside. Mabton said, "You damn fool. Come on." He started toward the basement stairs.

Ryne said, "Why did they quit? Why didn't they attack me?"

"Just be glad they changed their minds." Mabton let Ryne go first and paused behind him to swing the wall panel closed. "What did you think you were doing, going into the open that way?"

"I needed more exercise than I can get down here," Ryne said. "I'm ready to leave this place."

"Tara says you aren't," Mabton answered. "But that doesn't matter any more. You as good as told the Bully Boys and Wardens where you're hiding. We'll have to leave whether you're fit or not."

"They already knew," Ryne said. "The Bully Boys were waiting for me. So were the Wardens."

Mabton swore softly but made no comment. He led the way past the room where Ryne had lain so long and on to the end of the hall. Here he crouched, lifting a threadbare piece of carpet and then a square meter of flooring. Taking a hand torch from his pocket, he slashed the light down into darkness.

"Go down the ladder," Mabton said. "It's a long climb, so take it slow."

Even with the light from Mabton's torch, Ryne could see only a short distance down. He backed onto the ladder and began climbing, easing one foot after the other carefully. Now and then he looked down, able to see more as his eyes grew accustomed to the dimness. Finally he made out the floor, and then he was standing on its slightly curved surface. When Mabton joined him with the torch, Ryne saw that they were in a great tube, over two meters across and lined with stained and very old ceramic material.

"This is one of the drains from the original one-level City," Mabton said. He started forward, making Ryne take quick, long strides to keep up.

Ryne wondered where this tube led. If it was what Mabton claimed, then they were far beneath the streets of Lower City, beneath even the streets of that first one-level City.

Ryne said, "Why don't we use the old streets? That's the way the Listeners used to get to our place to hear my grandfather read."

"We did at one time," Mabton said. "But the Wardens know how to get to them. They've set trip alarms on every corner. All we can do is use these old tunnels."

"Does this lead to the Out?"

"Not this one," Mabton answered. "It was blocked off when the second City was built. We have to go up and then down again to reach the tunnel that used to connect to the spaceship. When the High destroyed what was left of it, they sealed all the tunnels too." He slowed and turned, his grin showing in the light from his torch. "But what's been sealed can be unsealed. Now save your breath and come on."

Ryne found that Mabton was right. He needed all of his breath and energy. He began to sweat under his clothing, and his muscles started to tremble from exhaustion.

Mabton kept him moving, slowing the pace a little but not stopping. They came to another ladder. This one went up; and to Ryne the climb seemed interminable. Finally he lay panting on the dust-covered floor of the cavernous building where he had met Weir and Tara.

Mabton remained silent until Ryne's breathing became more normal. Then, gently, he helped Ryne to his feet and led the way across the cavernous room to a rusting tank on the far side.

"From here we follow the route Weir and Tara used that day they met us."

Ryne remained silent, knowing now that he had to conserve all of his strength. Opening a door in the tank, Mabton led the way to its center. A manhole opened to darkness. Another ladder, Ryne discovered wearily. They climbed down to a tunnel similar to the one they had first come through.

"Last climb," Mabton said cheerfully. "All downhill walking from here on."

Once Mabton moved a bit too fast, stumbled, and momentarily lost the torch. For the first time in his life Ryne experienced true darkness. Always he had known light. In the daytime it filtered through the great force dome protecting the City and was augmented by hidden diffused lighting. At night, light was muted, but always it was there. Even in his sleeping quarters and in the apartment he had shared with Linne there was always soft, dim light. This blackness reached out to press around him with tangible, frightening force. It seemed to have a physical presence, a touch and scent of its own. The shock of it stayed with him for some time.

Suddenly they were blocked by a solid wall of the same fused ceramic material that lined the tunnels they had come through. Mabton pressed against the wall and reached up, running his fingers back and forth until he found what he sought. He pressed and a curved piece of the wall swung out, wide enough for them to step through.

Darkness rushed at them. Darkness and air such as Ryne had never experienced. For a moment he was puzzled, uncomprehending. Then he realized that he was feeling cold.

"Keep moving," Mabton advised. "It won't last long."

Teeth chattering, Ryne followed Mabton and stood aside as he closed the opening. The cold made Ryne's muscles jerk in uncontrollable spasms. He had difficulty in following the smaller man. Now they moved across a different kind of footing, through a different kind of tunnel. This had walls of man-hewn stone. It was narrow, barely accommodating Ryne's wide shoulders. The floor beneath his thin boot soles was rough, and more than once he stumbled awkwardly.

Now and then they passed strange-looking pieces of some rough, brownish material. Rectangular in shape, it ran from the floor up the walls to meet pieces of the same material pressed parallel to the roof. Ryne put his hand on one and drew it back, feeling a sharp, sudden pain lance his fingertip.

"What the devil is that?"

"Natural wood," Mabton said. He stopped and flashed the light on Ryne's finger. "You picked up a splinter." He nipped it out of Ryne's flesh. "Suck your finger," he advised. "It won't hurt long."

He laughed at Ryne's bewildered expression. "Genuine wood, from real trees—naturally grown trees bigger and more beautiful than any pictures you ever saw, then anything you could imagine."

Ryne made no answer and Mabton cocked an eyebrow at him. "Still find it hard to believe in the Out being livable?" Ryne nodded, and Mabton added, "Just how do you picture it?"

"Ice and snow in some places and burning desert and not too much air to breathe," Ryne said, as if he was reciting a lesson he had learned long ago in school. "That's why the ship that brought our ancestors built the City, to protect us from the terrible climate and the wild beasts."

"You have a lot to learn," Mabton said. "But then we all did once."

He moved on. The tunnel made a sharp turn, narrowed slightly, and then opened into a natural room, high-vaulted, its air damp and cold. On the near wall, hanging on pegs of wood, were strange-looking garments. Mabton pawed through them and finally handed one to Ryne.

"This might fit. Put it on and you'll be a lot warmer."

He took one for himself. "Watch how I do it." Lifting the garment, he slid into it by putting the bottom opening over his head. A hood that hung down the back of the garment he brought up to cover all of his head and face, leaving only a small opening for his eyes and nose.

Ryne followed suit. The garment was heavy and stiff and had a strange animal odor. But Mabton had been right; he could feel the protective warmth of it holding the heat of his body in. Following Mabton's actions, Ryne worked his hands through the ends of the sleeves and into two cumbersome mittens tied there.

The garment reached to Ryne's knees. "What is it made of?" he wondered.

"Wool," Mabton said. "It's made from sheep fur. It's called a parka."

"Sheep! I've seen pictures of them. They're Earth animals."

"The colony ship brought more than human embryos in its vaults," Mabton said. "There were those of all the animals useful to man—horses, and cows, dogs, cats, sheep, goats, several kinds of birds. Most of them adapted and survived. A few are even said to have crossbred with native fauna. But they're wild. I've never seen one."

Ryne tried to recall the pictures he had seen of all those kinds of animals, but they formed a confusion in his mind. He could recall that sheep were heavily furred, but he couldn't remember their size or appearance.

Mabton pointed to a row of clumsy-looking, high-legged boots lining the wall beneath the parkas. "Find a pair to fit over your own boots. They'll keep your feet warm."

Ryne located a pair and managed to squeeze his feet into them. They pinched a little, but like the parka they were warming. The tops came to the bottom of the parka. When Mabton clumped away, Ryne followed awkwardly. It took him a few moments to learn to walk in the boots, but finally he managed a respectable gait.

The passageway narrowed again and then, abruptly, it ended. Ryne stopped as if he had slammed into a wall of force. There was no longer the protection of rock on either side of him, nor above his head. There was just more cold air, sharper than any he had felt before, and before him a sight that held him motionless.

He was unaware of the cold, of Mabton standing beside

him, patiently waiting. His eyes were too filled with what they looked at to notice anything else. He had seen enough pictures to know that the purplish darkness above him with its great sweep of pinpricked light, unformed to his eyes—to know that he was looking at the sky. And at the stars.

Fear rose and was washed away by a great exultation. First he thought, "I'm in the Out!" And then he thought, "I'm free!"

He shouted the words aloud and the sound rolled away in the darkness and then faintly but distinctly returned to him. He turned his head slowly and looked at Mabton. Both smiled.

VIII

As Ryne stood motionless, letting the icy air cut like tiny knives at his face, a glow began on his left. It was far away and at first he was puzzled. Then it strengthened, spreading across the sky toward the zenith and fanning out along the horizon. A great orange-white globe vaulted into view. It moved with astonishing swiftness into the vault of the night, blotting out the stars with its brightness. Ryne could see it stretching a path of silver across a strange, lightly rippling surface.

His fear drained away under the impact of beauty he could not describe in words. His mind went back to pictures he had seen in old books, to the illustrated stories and the films of the ancient homeland—the almost mythical Earth.

"The moon!" he breathed.

"The hither moon," Mabton said. "The nether moon follows in an hour or so." He lifted a hand to the starred canopy above them. "One of those might even be the sun old Earth moves around," he said. It was one of the few times Ryne ever heard awe in Mabton's voice.

"When the moon gets higher," Mabton said, "you'll be able to see the trees. Living, growing wood in its natural state. And if you hold your breath and listen hard, you can hear the little night animals scurrying around in the forest."

Now Ryne was able to make out vague shapes around him. They had come into the open on a steep slope. As the moon threw brighter light, Ryne saw that a great mass filled the sky behind them, its edges outlined by a softer glow than that from the moon. It was, Mabton said brusquely, the glow from the City. Glancing downhill, Ryne realized that what had been dark vertical blotches were trees. He could make out the faint line of a cleared pathway twisting into them.

"We can't stand here all night," Mabton said. But there was no sharpness in his voice. "It got me the same way the first time. It still gets me every time I leave the City. But come on or we'll freeze."

Ryne followed him carefully down the steep path. Mabton spoke only once to say, "Watch for roots and rocks under your feet. This is a forest path, not a City walkway."

The path twisted. Now it was smooth under Ryne's thick boots; then it was rough and he almost tripped. After that he was more careful, keeping his eyes on Mabton's feet as much as on the surrounding trees. Here and there they formed a canopy overhead, blotting out the brightening moonlight. Along other stretches, the hither moon shone down on them with a brightness that surprised Ryne. Somehow, he hadn't visualized moonlight as quite so bright. Nor, when he was able to see the moon directly overhead, had he imagined it so large, so close.

The steepness of the path tapered off and they broke out of the trees into a cleared space. Ryne saw his first grass and felt it crackle crisply under his boots. Ahead a dim light showed. As they walked closer to it, Ryne saw the outline of a strange vehicle. It was like a great box twice as long as it was high. It stood on massive wheels, and two restless animals appeared to be attached to its front end. Horses, Ryne thought, remembering the old stories. Or were they cows? His memories of earth animals was somewhat confused. Mabton cleared up his questions before he could ask them.

"That's a wagon. Tara drove it from the Farm, the place where we live. Those are horses in front. Except for our legs, they're the only motive power in the Out."

They went to the rear of the wagon. A cloth flap hung down there, covering a wide opening. Tara drew the flap back and let a short flight of steps drop down to the ground.

"I was getting worried."

"Ryne had to stop and admire the moon on the sea," Mabton said.

She stood aside to let them climb the steps. "How do you feel, Ryne?"

"Tired but alive," he said.

"He's lucky to be that," Mabton muttered. He went on past Tara and disappeared through another cloth flap that hung across the front of the box. Ryne looked about. The box was just one large room. A standard heat unit stood in the middle, a spouted kettle of water steaming on its top. Overhead bulbs gave dim but adequate light. Along one long wall was a bench. Tara motioned Ryne to it and he sat down gratefully.

"Take off your parka," she said. "It stays warm in here." She pulled up the steps and then dropped the flap over the rear opening. "Ready, Mabton."

Ryne stood up, pulled off his parka, and hung it on a peg next to one he assumed to belong to Tara. He dropped wearily back to the bench and stretched his hands toward the heat unit. Tara poured some of the steaming water into a small pot. Ryne could smell the astringent odor of tea. He wrapped his hands around the mug she handed him.

"I've never known cold before."

"None of us did until we came here," Tara said. She sat beside him. "It won't last much longer. This is the beginning of what the Outers call the spring season. The nights will be cool but the days will get warmer and warmer." She laughed. "If you can believe the Outers, we're going to have one more good snowstorm before spring is all the way here." She added, "Snow is lovely."

"I've seen pictures," Ryne said. He felt empty, lost in the newness, the immensity of all this.

Out of sight up front, Mabton called, "Move out! Up there!"

"Brace yourself," Tara warned. "Wagons don't ride like City vehicles."

They moved forward with a sudden lurch that almost cost Ryne his mug of tea. A second lurch was followed by a sharp swing to the right, and then the wagon settled down to giving them a rough but less jerky ride. Tara let herself relax.

She called, "Tea, Mabton?"

"I'll wait. It'd freeze out here tonight."

She settled down to her tea. "Rest all you can. You used up a lot of energy tonight."

Ryne tried to fit his body to the swaying of the wagon. They speeded up and began to jounce. "Trouble?" Tara called to Mabton.

"Not if we hurry," Mabton said. "It looks and smells like snow now."

Tara laughed. "Mabton sounds more like an Outer all the time. Now he's predicting the weather."

Ryne clutched the edge of the bench with one hand. "Who are these Outers? Where do they come from?"

"The same ship that brought your ancestors," she answered. She saw his skepticism and shook her head. "In school, you learned more myth than history, Ryne. Those who refused to live in the first City weren't destroyed by animals and the elements. Instead, they formed their own society here in the open. Most of them migrated away from this area, but there is still a small colony near where we live."

"What do they do to live?" he wondered.

"Raise food from the soil, grow animals for meat. In the little village, people make things to sell to others. A few fish in the sea."

The wagon made a wide swing and jolted to a stop. "We're here," Tara said.

Here, Ryne discovered, was a stretch of frozen ground that separated a huge, dark building from a long, low, rambling lighted structure. Both, he learned later, were built of tree logs.

Outside the wagon, Tara turned toward a lighted doorway. "Mabton will put horses in the barn." She lifted her face to a now dark sky, without moon or stars. "Mabton's right. It does smell like snow."

They hurried across the hard ground and into a room lighted by a single electric bulb dangling from a ceiling cord. The room was cool, shut from the rest of the house by a heavy door. Here they put their parkas on pegs and their boots beneath them. Tara led Ryne through the heavy door, down a corridor past darkened rooms, and into a long, narrow, softly lighted room. At the near end was a large table; at the other a number of chairs and couches. Three men sat facing an open fire, their feet stretched toward the flames.

Fear rose in Ryne. Fire was the most dreaded disaster in the City. Common sense checked him from bursting out with the traditional warning cry. This fire was somehow obviously contained by the blackened rock walls enclosing it on three sides. And the men were enjoying it, not trying to quench it.

They turned and rose, facing Ryne and Tara. Weir was the nearest man. He held out a strong hand. "You're earlier than we expected, but welcome."

Next to him was a slender, dark-skinned man somewhere between Ryne and Weir's ages. "Corso," he said briefly.

"I remember," Ryne said. "You were a Riser. After the raids, you were exiled to Lower City. You disappeared. We all thought you'd been beaten to death by the Bully Boys."

Corso nodded. "I'm the man. Only I had a better fate. Weir and the others who'd found the way to the Out rescued me."

He stepped back to let the third man come forward. Ryne needed no introduction to recognize Laszlo. The lean, bony features, the olive skin stretched taut by high cheekbones, the burning eyes—all were living versions of the photograph Ryne had seen in the Coordinator's office. The impact of this man in the flesh was greater than Ryne had imagined. He felt the contained ferocity, the dedication, as no picture or words could bring them to him.

Feeling the outstretched hand, hearing the deep voice say, "Laszlo. Sit down, Ryne. There will be food soon," Ryne knew that Laszlo wasn't just a man dedicated to the cause he espoused; he was a man dedicated to being dedicated. If it hadn't been this, it would have been something else. In the ancient days, he would have been a prophet or a proselytizing priest, a demagogue arousing the people against whatever he disapproved of. He could not live otherwise, Ryne thought. Dedication to a cause was his way of life; and it was consuming him.

Ryne took an indicated chair near Laszlo. The others went quietly away. Ryne's feet were still chilled and he found it pleasant to stretch them toward the open fire. At the same time, he found himself fighting down an instinctive dread of those flames.

Laszlo said, "You must have many questions."

"Too many to know where to begin."

"Then relax and rest and listen," Laszlo said.

Ryne listened, and in the next half hour he learned about wood as fuel and as building material. He learned how food was grown in the ground and fed to animals who provided meat. He learned that there were really two colonies of men in this part of the Out—some hundred Outers and fewer than thirty Exiles, mostly men. Right now except for those Ryne had met, the Exiles were away, preparing to farm the land, or in the Outers' tiny village, helping to improve the still-primitive cottage industries.

"These Outers rescued Weir and the others who escaped from the City after the raids," Laszlo explained. "They taught the City men how to live from the land as they do. In return, we're trying to help them improve their way of living. Soon you'll meet our nearest Outer neighbors— Amso and his wife. Then you'll understand Outers better."

A call to the meal interrupted him. Ryne found the food—genuine, nonsynthetic food—exciting. Under Tara's care he had had only bland soups and soft foods, but here were actual meats, fresh vegetables, breads baked from ground grain. And the very quantities were emotionally overwhelming. For the first time in his life, Ryne saw people actually help themselves to a second full plate of food. For the first time, he knew what it meant to have an overstuffed stomach.

The meal over, Ryne and Laszlo returned to the fire while the others disappeared to do what they called "readying up the kitchen." But now Laszlo was silent, moving only to lift his teacup to his mouth or to poke at the settling fire. By the time the others returned, it was down to coals, and Laszlo rose as if that were a kind of signal.

"Show Ryne his bunk," he told Weir. He moved away, disappearing through a door.

"I'll check the animals once more and then we might as well all go to bed," Mabton said. "It's been a long day."

Weir led Ryne to a room containing four bunks. Undressing, he lay on the hardest but most gratefully received mattress he could remember. He shut his eyes against the dim light filtering through the open door. He expected to fall asleep immediately, but he found himself wakening.

Soon the other men came into the room. "It's snowing like billy-o, just the way I said it would," Mabton muttered. "Tomorrow will be a hard day."

They were soon settled, and shortly Ryne could hear their heavy breathing and an occasional soft snore. The room was darker than Ryne was accustomed to and he found sleep difficult. Even when he grew used to the darkness, he could not sleep. He was grateful when the door opened and Tara called softly for him to come out.

He dressed quickly and joined her. She had thrown wood on the fire and now the flames leaped and cascaded over the walls, providing the only light. She said, "I couldn't sleep my first night. I didn't think you could. Especially when you must have heard Mabton say it's snowing."

She took him by the hand and led him through a door next to the fireplace and onto a covered veranda. Light coming from a window on their right let him see snow—great white flakes drifting down, blotting out everything. They came in soft silence, falling lazily, steadily and yet excitingly.

Ryne thrust out his hand and caught a fat flake. It melted before he could bring it close to his face. He laughed like a child. "Snow!"

"Wait until morning," Tara said. "Come in now. You aren't dressed for this cold."

Back inside, they sat near each other on a couch and stared at the fire. Ryne heard movement from that part of the house where Laszlo had gone. "Will we disturb Laszlo if we talk?"

"If you mean waken him, no. I doubt if he ever sleeps over a few minutes at a time. Usually in the morning I find him slumped over his desk rather than in his bed," Tara said. "He'll be working, so let's keep our voices down."

A mixture of tenderness and exasperation crept into her

tone. "He's burning himself up. But that's the way he's been since I knew him. I don't expect to change him."

Ryne glanced at her. "You've tried?"

She gave him a faint smile. "Once, when we first met—in the High. But never very hard. I think I've always been too much under his spell to do anything but what he asked me to."

"Do you miss the High?" Ryne asked. He found himself wanting to know a great deal about this woman, yet fearing to make himself obvious.

"I miss the comforts sometimes," she said. "Things I took for granted. But there are compensations here—and they grow on you. And there's the satisfaction of what we're trying to do."

"How close are you to getting it done?" he asked.

"So close that once you provide the final piece, the puzzle will be solved."

"If I can," Ryne said. "I keep thinking, but I remember so little."

"You'll have help here," she said. "Books; the Outers, who use the old speech—in a way."

Ryne sat upright. "The Outers speak it? Then what's . . ."

She shook her head and touched his shoulder gently, settling him back. "They speak a very simple, almost primitive form of it, Ryne. And none can read or write it. They can't read or write at all." She rose to stir the fire. "I'll try to explain tomorrow when we go see Amso."

"What about the High people?" he persisted. "Don't they have books, micro-cards, other records of the old language?"

"No. Except for the Readers—except now for you—the art was lost. There's just nothing left to make a connection between the written symbols, the sounds, and the meanings of the words in the books we have. There aren't any dictionaries like we have for our tongue. Don't think Laszlo hasn't tried to decipher it. Until he finally agreed that you had to be brought down, he spent most of his time trying. We've all tried. We just haven't the basic knowledge."

She put a hand on his arm. "Don't downgrade yourself

too much, Ryne. Somewhere in your mind is knowledge you can bring to the surface."

"I'll try," he said. "But I recall so little. And I learned so few words when I was a child. . . ."

She leaned closer and brushed her finely shaped mouth against his lips. "Don't sound so despairing." Rising, she held out her hands. "Try to sleep now. Tomorrow Laszlo will want to talk in earnest. And he can be very exhausting."

Ryne returned to his bunk. He lay long awake, his mind turning her remarks over and over. His last thought before exhaustion forced him to sleep was a disturbing awareness of Tara as a person, as a woman.

IX

The snow-soft landscape that stretched from the front of the house to the bluff dropping down to the sea held Ryne from his wakening shortly after dawn until the odors of breakfast drove him from the veranda to the warmth of indoors. This was the Out! This cold beauty, this richly fresh gently moving air, this tang of natural foods, this—everything.

He shook a little from excitement and from anger at those who had cheated him of years when he could have known this, experienced it. And then he laughed at himself, at the absurdity of his thoughts. Coming to bring him to breakfast, Tara found him laughing.

"The snow did that to you?"

"Hardly." He told her, and she laughed too. "I know. I fell in love with the Out when I'd been here less time than you." She smiled up at him. "But you never fall out of love with it, Ryne."

"I'm scared at the same time," he said.

"It has its dangerous moments," Mabton said, coming up beside them. "You'll probably meet some soon enough."

After a meal that nothing in his childhood reading nor in his imagination had prepared him for, Ryne went off with Laszlo, through a heavy door and into the room that obviously served as office and sleeping quarters. A narrow cot sat against one wall, a clothes press that seemed to contain almost everything but clothes, and a washstand were the only concessions Ryne could see to Laszlo's living needs. Otherwise, there was a desk overflowing with books, a table littered with scattered drawings, another table filled with scribblings on sheets of paper—and everywhere more books, more papers. On the walls were maps that Ryne recognized as showing the ancient tunnels and streets of the original City and the more modern tunnels and streets of present Lower City. And there was one schematic drawing that required a few moments to puzzle at before he recognized the Power Core that burrowed deep into the earth.

"Sit down," Laszlo said in his peremptory way. "We have to talk."

Ryne sat down. Laszlo paced back and forth in the clutter of the room. "Did you have trouble with the Coordinator? How did you get him to exile you so quickly?"

There was suspicion here. Ryne had half expected it. Laszlo was a man who could see conspirators easily. And Ryne had thought about this and about a way to handle it. He followed his plan now, frankly detailing to Laszlo everything he and the Coordinator had said to one another.

Laszlo spent some time considering what he had heard. He said finally, "So as far as the Coordinator is concerned, you're his agent."

"Yes."

Laszlo smiled, a meaningless motion of his lips. "He lied to you, Ryne. He knows what the plan is—the big plan to build another City, to take the Lowers into it, to let them live there as human beings were meant to live—free to have the good of both the City and the Out."

Ryne was puzzled. "Then why would he send me? Why would he tell me to do what you wanted—read the Book that will let you do this?"

Laszlo said, "There's one part of the plan the Coordinator doesn't know, that he can't know. That's what he sent you here to discover."

He considered his own words and nodded. "Don't you see? The Coordinator doesn't yet know how we plan to move the Lowers from the present City to the new City—how we plan to get them through gates that have been tightly sealed for centuries.

"And he can't know that because I haven't got the complete answer myself. I will have by the time the new

City is ready, but up to now I haven't even discussed the problem with anybody."

"I don't see . . ." Ryne began.

Laszlo waved him to silence. "The Coordinator knows that we're preparing to take some kind of action. Weir and Corvo and some of the others have been organizing Lowers into groups. They meet frequently with the group leaders to keep them encouraged. The Coordinator has too many spies not to be aware of this."

He took a deep breath. "Isn't it clear? The Coordinator wants you to put me into a position where I have to reveal the plan to get the people through the gates. Once he knows what that plan is, then he can take steps to stop us.

"Can't you see what would happen if we started to put our plan in motion and the Coordinator with his Wardens and Bully Boys and Auxiliaries had anticipated us—and caused us to fail? The people of Lower City would be treated even worse than they are now. If we were allowed to live—if the very ones we're trying to help didn't destroy us out of frustration and rage—we'd be discredited. Our new City would sit where we built it, useless and empty."

Ryne nodded slowly. That would be the way the Coordinator thought. He said carefully, "But as long as I don't go running to him once the plan is known to me, then we should be safe enough."

"As long as you—or others who learn of it—don't go to him, yes. Then we're safe."

"Others?"

"Do you think you're the only agent the Coordinator has tried to send? There are others. There must be. He knows too much of what goes on here. . . ."

"The very fact that Weir and Corso have gone into Lower City and organized some of the people there has told him a lot," Ryne said. "He's no fool. And he has spies all through Lower City. He picks up rumors and adds them together. He—"

"That too," Laszlo said. "But there must be information coming from here as well. I don't know who or how. I just know it's true."

He turned abruptly away and then back. "But let's get to the immediate business—your reading the old language." He went to the clothes press. From it, he drew a metal box. Carrying it to the nearest table, he set it down almost reverently. "Do you recognize this, Ryne?"

Ryne was on his feet, opening the box. "My grandfather's," he said in a whisper. He lifted out six small books, their bindings stained, but the print on plasti-paper as clear and well remembered as ever. "My learning books! My story books!" He lifted out a notebook filled with grammatical exercises in his own hand. Beneath it he found the thick, heavily bound Book. "The Book." His fingertips stroked it, feeling the pebbly grain of the binding. He opened it and looked at the flyleaf, with his grandfather's name the twelfth of a list of Readers who had used it and passed it on. Each of the names had one thing in common: the single word Ryne.

"Can you read any of the Book?"

Ryne studied the title page. Slowly his lips formed the sounds represented by the symbols. He worked silently for some time before he read aloud the writing, the long-unused sounds coming not too easily but well from his tongue. "I think I can still read the very first part—but not very well."

"Let me hear," Laszlo said.

Ryne tried. Some of the words, some phrases, entire sentences came with surprising ease as he felt once again the unique rhythm of the old speech. Soon he began to sense word meanings rather than having to grope for them. Only when he sought to translate for Laszlo did he find himself stumbling. Stopping, he silently reread the opening passage, concentrating now on translating in his mind.

He said aloud, "I read it this way: 'No man shall hold another in thrall, for it is against the Will of the One. It is not for any man to set himself above other men, for that is mockery of the One, who created all equal by His Hand.' "

Pausing, he turned the page, his eyes seeking. "I remember this passage too: 'To deny a man food for the mind or for the body is equally as evil as to deny him freedom for the mind or for the body. Both are interdicted by the One.' "

"You're doing well," Laszlo said.

"I'm just finding places that impressed me as a child,"

Ryne said. A few pages on, he paused and read again: " 'From this City shall go the oppressed, led by the Hand of the One. Those who remain shall be called the Accused and shall labor as beasts. They will know hunger and want; they will live as they once forced the oppressed to live. It is they who have denied the One.' "

Laszlo was breathing heavily. "You aren't making that up, Ryne?"

"No. The Book is filled with passages like those." Ryne closed it gently. "Grandfather once told me that it is really a commentary of man's relation to man throughout history—from the beginning of history to the time of the first Reader, the one who wrote the Book during the long space voyage."

"Not just from the beginning of history to the time when the Book was written," Laszlo said, "but to the present." His eyes lighted with a half-wild fire. "And let's hope that history will stop here—in our time!"

He moved restlessly away and back. "It's frightening, Ryne. That last passage—almost as if the writer knew what the future would bring."

Ryne said, "Grandfather used to tell the Listeners that someday much of what the Book predicted would come true—and the Reader would be the instrument to bring about those truths." He sought to keep his voice level, to keep Laszlo from thinking he was being sarcastic.

"But I don't think I'll be the Hand of the One in this case, Laszlo. It won't be I who leads them from the City."

Laszlo was drawn, his taut flesh drained of color, his jaw muscles jumping visibly. He said, "Tonight, I want you to read those passages to the others."

When he spoke again, his voice was harsh. "You recalled much in a short time. Now tell me, how much of this book can you read?"

He brought a heavy volume from his desk, twice the length and breadth and thickness of the Book. He set it before Ryne and opened it to the title page.

Ryne stared at the large, stylized print. His lips formed the sounds, but when they echoed inside his head none held meaning for him. "No," he said. "Not yet."

Laszlo impatiently opened the book to a place where a small sliver of wood marked a section. Ryne stared at the two pages, that on the left consisting of two columns of fine print, that one the right a full-page highly technical drawing of what was obviously some kind of machine.

Ryne let his eyes roam down the printed columns. "I can read the small words, the common ones. But there are others that have no meaning at all. I'm not even sure I can sound them right."

Laszlo's eyes were feverish. "But you'll be able to figure out the words and their meanings! From the roots! From the context! From—"

"From a dictionary," Ryne said dryly. "I could do it if I had one. But not by the other means you suggested. I never learned the language by its roots, Laszlo. I learned it by rote and by speaking simple sentences with my grandfather and my father."

"There is no dictionary," Laszlo said. "Weir has looked."

"Looked where?"

Laszlo touched the small pile of books that had come from the box. "Where he got these; where he hid them the night of the raid. In your grandfather's house."

"Grandfather had more books—I remember almost a dozen, and one of them was a dictionary. But when he went to read, he took only the box. These are the books he always kept in it. Unless his other books were found and destroyed, they could still be there in the old house."

"Hidden?" Laszlo demanded.

"Hidden," Ryne said. "Everything to do with his being a Reader was carefully hidden."

"And you know where the hiding place was?"

"If I could stand in his room again, I think I could remember," Ryne said.

Laszlo nodded. "Then soon you'll go back to the City." He met Ryne's gaze. "Are you afraid? You could be caught."

"But I think the Coordinator gave orders to leave me alone."

"That's fine for those who've heard the orders, or those who accept them," Laszlo said. "But Bully Boys aren't always the most obedient animals."

Latest U.S. Government
tests of all cigarettes
show True is
lower in both
tar and nicotine
than 99% of all other
cigarettes sold.

Think about it.
Shouldn't your next cigarette be True?

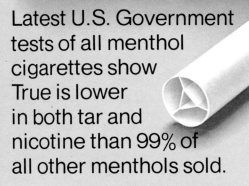

Latest U.S. Government
tests of all menthol
cigarettes show
True is lower
in both tar and
nicotine than 99% of
all other menthols sold.

Think about it.
Shouldn't your next cigarette be True?

X

In the days that followed, Ryne learned a great deal. Mabton and Weir and Corso taught him how a farm worked, taking him to meet the other Exiles working the fields or tending small herds of cattle and horses scattered throughout the long, flat valley the Outers had given Weir and the other settlers.

From Tara and Laszlo, Ryne unlearned the half-myths he had been taught in school and replaced them with truer history. And through his own efforts each night, he began to rebuild his knowledge of the simple elements of the ancient speech.

He was surprised to learn that the old tongue had once been the common speech of the City, as a form of it still was in the Out. But, as Laszlo explained, some three centuries after the first colonists from Earth crash-landed on this world and built their City, those who became the Highs arrived. They too had Earth ancestors, but while their ship was in its eighth century of seeking a world to colonize, two factions formed. The smaller, a group composed mostly of scientists seeking to establish a technocracy, had lost. They tried to take over by force and were defeated. Unceremoniously they and their families were put into two large lifeboats and set adrift. Staying together, they managed to survive until they landed here.

Laszlo spoke of it unemotionally at first, but as his recital went on, Ryne felt his intensity, his passion grow, and finally Laszlo stood before him, his mannerisms those of a speechmaker.

"They were ruthless people, those who became the

High. They had planned to take their ship and rule it. They followed the same scheme here. They were—and remain—believers in much for the few and in little for the many. Their basic criteria for judging who shall be among the few was intelligence. And that they defined as those wise enough to accept their view. That view was right and good; anything else was wrong and evil."

The Highs turned quickly from the Outers, realizing that little was to be gained by conquering a people with a technological level too low to raise easily. But those in the City gave them the opportunity they wanted. Bearing gifts of improved technology, they were welcomed. They took their time, integrating slowly into the already dichotomized culture of the City, feeling their way until they knew the psychologies of the people they dealt with. Then they simply eased themselves into a position of leadership.

Laszlo stared at Ryne with clenched fists. "That both Uppers and Lower revolted against them mattered not at all. They had control of the technology, and they were ruthless. But no small group of demagogues can stand long against a mass fifty times their size. Finally peace came through the compromise—mostly in favor of those who became the Uppers—the ones who had been in positions of command in the original City. The revolts had pretty well destroyed it, and the Highs used the machine to build the present City with its three levels on the rubble of the old."

From Tara Ryne learned the further history of the City he had always taken so for granted. A following generation of Highs, faced with a threat by the Lowers and some of the Uppers to build themselves a City elsewhere, acted with far greater repression than had those who preceded them.

"That's how Laszlo found out about the machine," Tara explained to Ryne. "Its description—but unfortunately not its operation—is still in the High archives. After the last revolt, the Highs deliberately went into the Out. They destroyed the remains of the original ship, assuming that they had also destroyed the machine and its power source along with any records left by the first colonists. Then they sealed the City, closing the great gates and stopping any intercourse between Outers and City dwellers. As a final step they repressed the use of the old speech by Uppers or Lowers and forced their own language onto everyone."

Until that time, Ryne learned, the Lowers spoke the old tongue and the Uppers were mostly bilingual, depending on their relationship to the High superstructure. The Highs disdained to speak what they considered the crude tongue, preferring their own language. Through education and destruction of books and of micro-cards with the old writing, in a century they had replaced the old language with a mode of thought and communication more suited to their desires.

Except, Ryne remembered, for the Readers. Once respected men in the community, the Readers had gone underground during the first revolt. Following the decree making use and finally even knowledge of the old tongue a criminal offense, they had burrowed deeper into the old City for refuge, their followers growing fewer with each passing generation, and finally there was only one Reader.

Tara's explanation came while she and Ryne were taking his first buggy ride, following a road across the valley to low hills separating it from the nearest area inhabited by Outers. He turned from watching the sea glitter under a warm spring sun.

"If the High destroyed the machine, how can Laszlo build a new City?"

"Because of a bit of irony," Tara said. "To understand what happened, we have to go back to the early history of colonization of this world. When the first ship crash-landed—burying itself in that mountainside that separates us from the City—two distinct groups emerged: those who wanted to live in the open and those who wanted the protection of a City, the nearest thing they could get to the cocoon of the ship that had encased them and the generations before them. So the original City was built for some; others moved to where we're going and built their own settlement.

"At first there was easy intercourse between the two groups. But then the Outers developed a Messiah—a man who preached that the City and its technology, its enclosing itself away from nature, were evil. That the only true good was the good of nature. History on Earth has many instances of a strange idea taking hold of a given community and engulfing it. That happened among the Outers. The technology they had was deliberately destroyed. Even their buildings were razed. When they rebuilt, they had to cut logs from trees by hand, haul the logs with horses, and make log buildings like the farm. Later they dug ore from those mountains you can see off to the east. They smelted it and worked it in primitive forges to make their tools. It was a kind of madness that lasted for over two centuries. The end result was a people virtually living backwards as far as cultural progress is concerned.

"A few rebelled and went to the City, but most of them returned, preferring the Out to living under a force dome. But in the City they had seen what labor technology could lift from a man, and they formed a rebel group to stand against the current Messiah. Finally, there were two groups. Those who followed the Messiah migrated northward, away from the hated City. The rebels stayed.

"But they were pitifully few," Tara said. "Even now they number only in the hundreds, and most of those are in the village. At first they tried to renew their contact with the City, but the big revolt had come and it was sealed against them. Then they attempted to revitalize their technology, but what they had to draw from was almost nothing. Too many years had passed, too many generations who knew only their particular Messiah's concept of civilization lay between the time when they had a technology and the time of their rebellion.

"Most devastating was the tampering with the language. That began with the first Messiah and was carried on ruthlessly by his successors. They kept the old tongue but they destroyed all writing as unnatural, as evil. Over the centuries, speech deteriorated to where, even now, it's on a purely basic level. When you hear it, Ryne, remember that. Don't expect anything more than the most elementary concepts for the most elementary needs. For example, when Weir and the others came, they brought electricity. The Outers no longer had a word for it; they had to borrow ours. And they are completely illiterate."

She stopped the horse at the top of the last rise to let it rest. With a wave, she indicated the valley spread out below, running hour-glass-shaped from distant mountains to sun-glittering sea. In the near distance, Ryne could see neatly rectangular fields set off by wooden pole fences. Beyond them clustered buildings that looked much like the Farm. And in the distance, where the land dipped to meet the tide, a group of buildings huddled together.

"The village," Tara said, pointing. "The nearest buildings are Amso's farm. When you meet Amso and his wife, you'll understand better what I mean about Outers."

Ryne braced himself as they started downslope. "About the machine . . ." he said.

"Didn't you think I'd ever get back to the subject?" she laughed. "When the rebels found themselves sealed off from the City, they turned to the only source for technology they knew—the original colony ship. They stripped it of everything they could carry or drag, hiding everything in the caves that riddle the mountainsides. The Highs destroyed the ship soon after, unaware that anything had been taken from it.

"A watchdog committee was set up to protect the things taken from the ship. This committee became a one-family affair. And only that family knew in which cave things were hidden. To make doubly sure, each generation of watchdogs moved everything to new caves. Amso is the present watchdog, and he's the only man on this planet who knows where the machine is."

"Does he know what it's for?"

"He has only a vague idea, even though Laszlo tried to explain it to him."

Ryne frowned. "But if Amso alone knows, how can Laszlo expect to get the machine and use it?"

"Amso took Laszlo to see it once," she said. "That's when Laszlo began developing his plan. Later, Amso moved everything again. But he's agreed that when we need the machine, he'll take us to it."

"I assume that suits Laszlo," Ryne said heavily. "He must feel safer with it so well hidden."

She glanced at him. "He told you too about what he calls the 'Coordinator's Agents'?" She hesitated and added in a low voice, "Laszlo is very important to me, very dear, but I recognize his faults."

"Then you don't think there are agents?"

"There may be, but I refuse to be as paranoid about it

as Laszlo." She shrugged. "Still, it is comforting to know that the machine is safe until we need it."

There were trees on the slope, and she pulled into the shade of the last stand before the clean valley land took over. She turned to Ryne. "Laszlo told me about you and the Coordinator. He wants to believe that you're with us, but being Laszlo, he—well, he isn't sure."

"How do I convince him?" Ryne demanded. "If I'm not able to read the book, he'll think I'm against him. If I do, he won't be sure I'm not doing what the Coordinator wants."

She nodded. "And he won't be sure until it's all over. Until we're in the new City and he's seen how you've helped." She looped the reins around the handle of the buggy whip and turned to him. Her hands rested lightly on his upper arms. "Ryne, how sure are *you*?"

"I always was sure," Ryne said. "For a time some of my beliefs got buried under the layer of fat the Uppers and Highs buried my mind under—with their security. That's all gone. It's been gone for some time."

"Since you met your Linne?"

"That washed away the last of it," he admitted.

"She's terribly important to you, isn't she?"

The tone of her voice bothered him, as did her nearness, her strong beauty. He said thickly, "As important as Laszlo is to you."

Her mouth curved upward in a smile. "Did you think Laszlo was my—what is your Upper term, 'pair-up'? Hardly. Laszlo has no time for such things. I'm my own woman, Ryne; I work with Laszlo because I believe in what he's doing, not out of some blind idolatry."

Ryne said, "There's none of that between Linne and me either. We're just compatible. We like being together. If that's love, then we're in love."

She lifted one hand and let her fingers touch his cheek. "And even without her, you'd be sure?"

"Yes," Ryne said.

"And you aren't afraid—of what you might lose? Of failure? Of what might happen to you, to us, to Linne, if we should fail?"

"Yes," Ryne said. "I'm scared as hell sometimes."

XI

They were silent until they swung into the area between Amso's solid house and his series of connected barns. Amso himself came from the nearest barn, a blacksmith's hammer swinging from one strong hand. He was a man in middle age, his face roughened by contact with the weather. Hard-jawed, not given much to smiling, he still seemed to Ryne pleasant and open and someone he would want for a friend rather than an enemy.

His handclasp was strong as he greeted them. He spoke their tongue, but slowly with a definite heavy accent. "I heard you were coming," he said to Ryne. "Come in and we'll talk about what interests you."

Inside, Ryne met Mrs. Amso, as everyone, including her husband, called her. A tall woman, rawboned, of a type Ryne had never met, she was working over a wood-burning stove that filled the large kitchen with pleasant warmth. She had a smile for them, and then without apparent effort, a pot of strong tea and something Tara identified as deep-dish fruit pie with skimmed cream for a topping.

"Hot from the oven," she said to Ryne.

"It smells wonderful," he answered. He dipped in his spoon. "And tastes even better," he added when his mouth was empty.

Amso chuckled. "Listen to them, would you? The old speech rolls out of him like he was an Outer."

Tara laughed at Ryne's startled expression. He hadn't realized until now that Mrs. Amso had used a rather oddly accented but understandable form of the ancient tongue and that he had responded in kind.

"You see," Tara said, "you'll be able to do it."

"The talking will help, for all that we haven't many of the words you'll need," Amso said. "Spend a few days in the village and hear nothing else, and you'll be thinking in the good words again."

"Amso and a half-dozen other men learned our tongue from Weir," Tara explained. "They needed it to understand the little technology we've been able to give them and that they have the materials to make use of."

Amso waved proudly to the electric bulb hanging from the ceiling. "There's that and a motor to pump our well water and such things. And when the new City is built, we'll have the machines that book of Laszlo's shows— machines to plow the soil and harvest the crops, to saw the wood."

They talked disjointedly, not in City speech, occasionally in the old tongue for the benefit of Mrs. Amso, though then Tara was left out. Ryne learned more about how a man lived from the soil, about the rhythm of the seasons, and he got a glimpse of the constant, unrelenting labor that tied a man to the land.

"But once we get the machines, then there'll be time for a little living too," Amso said. He repeated the words in the old tongue for his wife. She smiled and nodded and offered them more food.

Tara declined with a laugh. "We only came for you to meet Ryne and to ask about his spending some time in the village. And to get some cream," she added.

"I'll see to his staying in the village, whenever he chooses to come," Amso said. "As for the cream, I'll get it now. And come along to see the new calf, Tara." He grinned at Ryne. "You might tell Mrs. Amso about the City. She has a powerful curiosity."

Alone with Mrs. Amso, he drank more tea and haltingly tried to give her a verbal picture of life under the great dome. She had never been closer to it than Laszlo's farm; and she was only aware of it from talk and because of the glow it cast against the sky at night. Ryne found trying to explain a futile exercise, and he was relieved when Tara returned to take him away.

They drove back quickly, Ryne holding a heavy crock of cream between his legs. He thought about Amso. "He should be a good man to guard the machine," he said suddenly.

"Amso? A very good man," she agreed. "A strong-willed man."

"Does he know the use of any of the things in the cave?" Ryne asked.

"I doubt it." She cast him a curious glance. "What are you thinking of?"

"A dictionary," Ryne said. "A book or micro-cards. My grandfather had a dictionary. There must have been others."

"Laszlo said you were going to town soon to hunt for a dictionary."

He nodded. "But if I can't find it, I was thinking there might be one in the cave."

"It's something to remember," Tara agreed. "*If* you still need it after you spend some time in the village."

"If they have no more words than Amso, I'll need it," he said dryly.

He went to the village the next afternoon. Five days later he returned, riding his first horse proudly, alone, but with disappointment etched on his features. It had been an interesting five days. He had met many people he found congenial, and he had learned of an area of human life he had had no concept of before. He had seen the small cottage industry at work, had watched the blacksmith at his forge, had sat in on a town meeting where the problem of a new drinking-water source had been hammered out in mutual discussion. And he had worked, physically. All of this he told to his eager listeners at the supper table.

"The language, man," Weir interrupted. "What of the language?"

"I can speak on their level as though I'd been born to it," Ryne admitted. "But it's not as sophisticated a speech as I used with my grandfather. They're poverty-stricken, and for all my probing, none could recall any words useful to us."

He looked around the table and met Laszlo's gaze. "It'll have to be the dictionary or nothing."

"We'll go in the morning," Weir decided. He glanced

from one to the other of them. "I think we'll take horses right up to the tunnel."

"How many of us do you need?" Tara asked.

"Only Mabton, Ryne, and myself. Too many would be of no use."

"Then I'll go to Amso and talk to him about the things in the cave," Tara said. "In case you should fail." She smiled at Laszlo. "Unless you have something else for me to do."

"That's as valuable as anything," he said.

Later, alone with Laszlo, Ryne said, "I'm sorry I made no more progress." He added without thinking, "I hope you've done better with the last phase of the plan."

Laszlo's eyes burned at him. "Would you like me to tell you—so you could communicate it to the Coordinator once you reach the City tomorrow?"

Intellectually, Ryne realized, he was able to cope with Laszlo. But on the emotional level, he found himself helpless against his own anger. He rose from his chair, choking back a desire to curse the man. He finally managed to say, "If you have no more faith in me than that, why do you keep me around?"

"I have faith only in myself," Laszlo said. "If you're not guilty, you'll brush such remarks aside." He was stiff, unbending; yet he was, in his way, offering an apology. Even so, Ryne had to leave. He withdrew to the dining room, where he worked with the books to quicken his reading comprehension of the old tongue.

It was late when Weir found him there. "We leave early. Better get some sleep."

"When I'm sleepy," Ryne said shortly.

Weir cocked an eyebrow at him. "Laszlo been at you?" He grinned. "Last week he as good as accused me of having a secret transmitter with a direct line to the Coordinator." His big hand clapped Ryne's shoulder. "Come to bed, man. Laszlo is as he is. And most of what he says in that vein means nothing."

Agreed, Ryne thought, but what would Laszlo do if such thoughts stopped being meaningless to him, began to obsess him? Physically, Laszlo was no match for him, but then he doubted if Laszlo would fight with physical weapons.

The Coordinator studied the report on his desk and called his Secretary. "Ryne is coming to town. He might even be in the old City by now. Are you sure the Wardens got the message this time? He is *not* to be bothered."

"I'm sure," the Secretary said. "But I'll send a reminder down right away." As he turned to go, the Coordinator's peremptory voice stopped him.

"Have you finished that report on the female, Linne?"

"Today," the Secretary said. He frowned. "The risk of keeping her here in Upper City . . ."

"Is minor compared to the risk of our failing," the Coordinator said tartly. He tapped the report in front of him. "There's no question at all that Ryne has made his choice. We've lost him—if we ever had him."

"But if he should be the one we have to depend on to learn Laszlo's final plan . . ." the Secretary began.

"If he should be—and he most likely will be if he succeeds in translating the Book—" He tapped the report again. "If he should be, we know he won't report to us of his own volition. That's why the girl is still here, unharmed, being given such information as I choose to give her."

He leaned forward. "Try and use some imagination. Try and picture what Ryne will do when we let him know that his woman, his pair-up, is our prisoner, and that he can have her—safe—if he finishes the work he was sent to do."

"Does he feel that strongly about her?"

"He did," the Coordinator said. "I think he still does." He nodded. "But perhaps you're right. We could be sure with a test . . ." He broke off, staring at the wall behind the secretary. "Today," he said. "While Ryan is in the City."

Ryne was pleased with himself. He stood on the flat top of the great cylinder housing the power cables of the main utilities and grinned at Weir. They had come at a steady pace along tunnels, up ladders, across ancient, dim floors, and he still felt strong, his breathing easy.

"Do you know how to get there from here?" Weir asked.

"Hardly. I never went into these tunnels when I was a child."

Weir nodded. "We have to go into the open in one place," he said. "Be ready to move fast if I signal." He pursed his lips and gave a low whistle. "That means 'safe.' You can come on." He whistled at a higher pitch. "That means 'go back—right now!'"

He led the way into the big duct, along it a short distance, and then out into another of what seemed to Ryne to be an endless series of branch ducts. Finally they came to a ladder. Weir led the way up, pausing just below the street surface.

"Here's where we show ourselves. There's a good half-block before we can get out of sight again. Come right up behind me. Once I lift this cover over my head, we have to move fast."

Ryne moved up to stand with his head one rung below Weir's feet. Weir said, "Now," and thrust upward. Light oozed in around them, along with the stench of Lower City. He disappeared with a flick of his legs. Ryne followed, pulling himself up onto the paving of a grimy street. He thought he saw movement some distance away, but it was not repeated; otherwise there was no sign of life.

Weir replaced the cover of the manhole and started swiftly toward the nearest corner. Ryne strode behind him. Once around the corner Ryne stopped, turned, and flattened himself against the building wall. Then carefully he eased back just enough to see around the corner. A Warden vehicle was at the far end of the street they had just left. It came toward them, but slowly, almost leisurely.

Weir whistled softly, the pitch low. Ryne turned and motioned to him. "Wardens," he said.

Weir took a look and shook his head. "They don't act as if they're after anyone." He continued to watch. "What the devil are they up to, weaving that way from curb to curb?"

He pushed the question aside impatiently. "Let's move along before they do smell us out. It's that door in the old building in the middle of the block."

They were ready to cross the street to the building when

two Bully Boys sprang from an areaway just ahead of them. They were young, big, grinning with anticipation.

"Run for it," Weir snapped.

"From only two of them?" Ryne demanded. The expressions on their faces brought the anger surging up in him, as it always had. He could feel himself shaking with the desire to smash them down, to defeat them with the only argument they knew—brutal force.

"Two, hell!" Weir snapped. He jerked his head.

Coming from the door where they had expected sanctuary was another pair of Bully Boys, almost like twins to the others, with the same kind of faces. Weir swore sharply. A Warden vehicle slid around the far corner, blocking the street.

"A trap!"

Ryne said, "You take the pair across the street. I'll take these and join you inside."

For all of Weir's age, Ryne suspected that he could handle a pair of Bully Boys. He had seen Weir's strength more than once, and he knew that his own was the greater for his time in the Out.

He saw Weir move into the street, toward the pair on the other side. Purposefully he moved toward the two nearest him. Their grins grew tight. Ryne let his hands hang loosely at his sides, revealing nothing of his plan of attack. He was within two meters of them when they stopped.

One of them laughed. "No fight, Riser. Just a message. Your woman is in trouble."

Ryne stopped in midstride. "What the devil are you talking about?" His eyes moved past them to the Warden vehicle. It had stopped just past the corner.

"Your pair-up," the Bully Boy said. "Name of Linne." He jerked his head at the ancient building across the street. "Go see for yourself."

Ryne swore thickly at them. "If you've hurt her . . ."

"Now why would we do that?" the other one demanded. "We knew you'd be along sooner or later. We thought you might like to go after her—if you can reach her."

"Go on," the first one said. "Go on inside."

Ryne looked in Weir's direction. He was standing on the far sidewalk, his fists clenching and unclenching. The

Bully Boys were backing away from him. The door to the building was open. Weir was staring past them to the inside.

"Linne," he called to Ryne. "Linne's in there—with a dozen of these animals." His voice shook, rising. Ryne had never seen him without composure before.

"I heard," Ryne said. He swung around, facing the Bully Boys again. He moved at them suddenly. His hands reached out, catching an arm of each as they tried to turn and run. He spun them viciously together so that their bodies met. He let loose. One staggered back, holding a hand to his face where it had struck the other on the forehead. The second man stood shaking his head. Ryne came forward again. He hit the nearest one with his full strength, smashing him against the building at one side. He dropped and lay still. Ryne went after the other. He turned and ran, stumbling, staggering.

The Warden vehicle was moving forward now. Ryne changed his direction and charged directly at it. He could see the two faces under the uniform caps, and he saw surprise as he jerked open the driver's side door and hauled the man out. The Warden twisted free and swung up his club. Ryne caught his wrist and twisted. The Warden screamed as the bone snapped. Ryne caught the falling club and went headfirst into the vehicle, the club swinging.

He stopped, club in midair, as the Warden opened his door, scrambled out, and began to run. His partner, holding his broken wrist, followed. Ryne slid around on the seat until he was facing the front of the vehicle. He lifted the communicator from its hook.

A voice said, "Warden Central."

Ryne snapped, "Get me the Coordinator—now! The name's Ryne."

There was no discussion, no argument. A clicking sound and within seconds he heard the voice of the Coordinator. "Ryne?"

"Ryne," he agreed. "The Bully Boys have Linne down here in a warehouse. If you want your job done, see that she's taken away from them. What the devil kind of security system have you got, letting . . ."

The Coordinator's smooth voice said, "She's unharmed,

Ryne. And perfectly safe. She'll be back in Upper City in half an hour." He laughed without much humor. "I just wanted you to know what I can do if I have to. I don't want you to get any ideas from Laszlo. Do you understand me, Ryne?"

"I understand," Ryne said. Suddenly his shaking anger was gone. He felt a coldness, a deeper, quieter anger like a great ball of ice in his middle.

"You've been tested," the Coordinator said. "Go about your business."

He closed the circuit. Ryne hung up the communicator and turned. Weir stood just outside the vehicle.

Ryne said, "The Coordinator . . ."

"I heard. They took Linne away and then closed the door." Weir was looking at him with open curiosity. "You didn't think trying to play a double game would be easy, did you? You didn't take the Coordinator for a fool?"

Ryne shook his head and climbed slowly from the vehicle. Weir said, "The way you went after those Bully Boys and the Wardens—you must think a lot of Linne."

"Yes," Ryne said.

"What would you have done if it hadn't been a test?" Weir said. "If it had been genuine? Would you have given in to him?"

Ryne looked at him emptily. "I don't know," he said. "I don't know."

XII

No one disturbed them now. They went into the old building and down another ladder and worked their way through what seemed to Ryne to be a maze, although Weir was careful to explain the markings that told him when to turn left, or right, or continue straight ahead.

At the end, they were in a cavernous room beneath the present City. The only light came from a big lamp such as Mabton had packed for Ryne during their journey through the tunnel. It was located so that it sprayed out to show the faces of the fifty or so men sitting in semicircular rows, and to light Ryne and Weir standing before them.

Ryne stood quietly as Weir asked for reports from each man. They came, succinct and to the point, and the gist of all was the same: Their lieutenants and the men beneath them had found few Lowers not willing to migrate, once they were given the slightest assurance of success.

Each of the men here, Weir had explained to Ryne, had charge of ten men, their lieutenants, and each of those in turn had charge of ten. And it was these ten who went among the people, questioning, talking softly, building the picture of the future that was so close to being reality.

Among those Lowers who held back their approval, Ryne learned, were many of the very old, and a goodly number of women, especially those with young children and employed husbands. Weir accepted this part of the reports as he had the other, with an expressionless nod.

He said, "That's understandable. As for the oldest, there's little we can do. Many will be too feeble to move. But the women are a different story. Have your men

88

identify them specifically. Have them talk to the husbands and try to get permission to move them and the kids bodily if we have to."

He took a deep breath and nodded his chin in Ryne's direction. "Here's the breakthrough I talked about at the last meeting. Here's the reason we're not feeling just hopeful any longer; now we're feeling sure of ourselves. This is Ryne."

One man in the second row said, "I heard about him. He's a Riser they exiled."

Weir jerked his head again and moved back. Ryne stepped forward. "That's right." He had a plausible, simple-enough story ready for this group. "I got myself exiled when I learned I was needed in the Out."

They waited, watching him, giving nothing to him yet, accepting nothing. Ryne said, "My grandfather was the last Reader." He heard the stirring, the rustling, the soft intakes of breath. "You all know the plan to build the new City. And you know that the machine this City was built with still exists. The problem is that the instructions for using the machine are in the old tongue. My grandfather taught me to read the old writing, and so they wanted me in the Out, to help them read the instructions for the machine."

He saw the hope on some faces, the doubt on others. He said, "The words in the book about the machine are different, but I'm learning them. Soon I'll be able to read enough so that the new City can be built."

"How soon is soon?" a voice called.

This was a question Ryne had faced in his own mind, and one he had not yet found an answer for. "I don't know," he admitted. "But I want it as soon as you. Sooner, perhaps. My—my woman is in Upper City. I want her with me." He looked at the rows of faces, moving his head slowly. "Many of you know her. She carries the name of Linne."

And now he saw more of them relax, come to him. He said carefully, "Tell the doubters, the skeptics, the frightened, that not many days ago I'd never seen the Out. But since then I've lived in it. I've been fed and housed and clothed by it."

He took a step forward. "I've seen the sun and felt its

warmth. I've seen the sea. I've breathed the air. Men live there, men whose ancestors come from the same ship as did yours. Men who are free. Tell the others this."

His emotional outburst had startled him and drained him. He stepped back, making room for Weir. He said simply, "Tell them about the sun."

The meeting broke up then, with Weir setting the next for a cycle ahead. Silently he and Ryne backtracked through the maze of tunnels, taking turns that Ryne did not recognize. Twice Weir hesitated and then went ahead firmly. He stopped at the foot of a ladder climbing up into darkness.

"We'll come up in front of your old house." He looked at Ryne in the backwash of the light from his torch. "Try to get the layout straight in your mind now. We might not have too much time. The people living there are dissenters."

"I can go in blindfolded," Ryne said. He started up the ladder.

The street was as he remember it, drab, the houses seemingly no more grimy than those many years ago. The familiar door surprised him a little: the big scar that had been put in the doorframe in the aftermath of the raid was still clearly visible. Somehow he had expected it to have been covered over by time.

As soon as Weir came up behind him, Ryne led the way to the door of the house. Whoever lived here now obviously complied with the law—the door was unlocked. Ryne entered the lower hall. "Straight back and to the left. We had this whole side of the lower floor." Three rooms, he remembered, for four people to eat, sleep, cook, relax. He started walking.

The door to the room yielded under his turning of the knob. The perpetual glow of the City came dimly through the single window into the unlighted room. A woman and a small child sat at a table eating. The woman stared at them with fear in her tired eyes.

"No one's going to hurt you," Ryne said. "I used to live here. I just came back to visit."

Behind him Weir stepped in and shut the door. He stood with his back to it. The woman swiveled her head silently as Ryne studied the room, making a slow clockwise turn. Some of the furniture was the same—the chairs and the table. But a larger bed had been put alongside the cot his grandfather had slept on, and there was no longer the familiar clothes press against the side wall.

"The clothes press," Ryne said, "what happened to it?"

"There wasn't no room," the woman said. Her voice was full. "Them next door took it. They give me clothes for the boy here. Old clothes."

"Then you never used it? Never opened it?"

She was frankly puzzled now. "We used it awhile, but there wasn't no room, so we traded it." She made a giggling sound. "You leave something in it?"

"Yes," Ryne said. He made a shape in the air with his hands. "A box. It was under the bottom board. In the little hollow space between it and the floor."

Ryne saw the crafty look flick into her eyes and then fade. "I seen that," she said. "Maybe we could swap."

Ryne glanced at Weir. His own pockets were empty of anything she might want. Weir showed her what his pocket held—two hand-hammered nails, a piece of wire, and a small washer he had been straightening with a hammer.

"This is all we have," he said.

The woman shook her head and touched her tongue to thin, bluish lips. "Them boots of his," she said, nodding at Ryne. "They'd about fit my man. He's small but he has big feet."

Without hesitating, Ryne removed his boots. "What do you have to swap for them?"

"We found the box when we was moving the press," she said. "I kept it."

Both Ryne and Weir saw her eyes flick toward the larger bed. Weir went to it and knelt. He reached beneath the bed and drew out a large flattish metal box.

"Now you wait," she said. "This is a swap."

"That depends on what's in it," Weir said. He lifted the lid and carefully began to bring out tattered clothing, a handmade toy, odds and ends that the woman had obviously saved over the years. "The books?"

"Ah, them. They wasn't no good to us in that funny writing. I got rid of them."

"Who'd you swap with?"

She was sullen. "I didn't get a swap. My husband was

scared, the fool. He said we could get in trouble because of the old man who used to live here. The crazy one. He called the Wardens. They took the books."

Ryne put his boots back on. The woman looked as if she was going to cry. Weir laid the nails and wire and washer on the table. "Show these to your husband. If he can't make use of them, they'll make a toy for the boy."

Silently he and Ryne went out. They were on the street before either man spoke. "Wardens," Weir said. "What would they do with them?"

"Report up to the Coordinator's office if they were wise," Ryne said. "He'd have taken them."

Weir said with heavy amusement, "Then call him again and ask him to lend you a dictionary."

Ryne said, "Why not? Where's the nearest communication center?"

"At the food dispensary around the corner," Weir said. "Don't ask for trouble. You'll have Wardens . . ."

"There won't be any trouble," Ryne said. "He has Linne."

Weir said only, "It's this way."

They started to the left. "I remember now," Ryne said and quickened his pace.

The shop was small, as all Lower City dispensaries were; there was little but the basic diet to be had in them. Inside, behind a counter with grillwork above it, was the lone attendant, a retired factory worker who had earned this position by years of faithful service. And, Ryne suspected, by being an agent for the Coordinator. Behind the attendant were the locked cases containing the food.

He looked from Ryne to Weir, and his eyes grew wide in his seamed face. He was old enough to remember Weir well, and the recognition and the shock were there. He scuttled to one end of the counter and reached beneath it for the communicator.

Ryne said, "Don't waste time calling the Wardens. Ask for the Coordinator. Say that Ryne wants to talk to him again."

The old man was breathing hard. "Ryne! You're crazy, coming out this way."

"Just call," Ryne said. He could see stubborn negation on the ancient features. "Don't get yourself in trouble by having the Wardens make a useless trip. They'll only call the Coordinator."

The old man squeezed his lips together and then said into the communicator, "This is District 5 food dispensary. Man here says his name is Ryne. He wants to talk to the Coordinator."

His head jerked away from the listening device. Muttering, he pushed the communicator through the grillwork to Ryne. "It's your trouble, not mine," he said.

Ryne took the communicator. The Coordinator was already on the other end. Ryne said, "Some years ago, the books belonging to my grandfather were turned over to the Wardens. One was a dictionary of the old and new languages. I need it."

"I'd forgotten," the Coordinator said. "But there was a Warden report . . ." He paused. "Wait."

Ryne stood listening to the faint hum through the communication line. He thought of Linne, and he turned so that neither Weir nor the old man could see his expression. Soon the Coordinator's voice came again. "I'm sorry, Ryne. The report says they received the books. That was fifteen years ago. They destroyed them and then reported."

"Is that the truth?"

The Coordinator clearly took no offense. "The truth. I'm as sorry as you. But you'll have to do without it."

"I'll need more time, then," Ryne said.

"Take what you have to have but no more." The line went dead.

Ryne returned the communicator. "The Wardens destroyed them," he said.

This time neither he nor Weir spoke until they reached Mabton at Utilities Central. "You're late," he said.

"There was a little trouble," Weir answered. He described everything that had happened as they made their way toward the Out.

Ryne could feel Mabton's eyes turned on him. He returned the look and saw the curiosity and the watchfulness. Mabton said, "What happens if he still has Linne and you need to make a choice, Ryne?"

"I was planning on going to Upper City and getting her out," Ryne said.

"No," Weir told him. "You can't. "You're too necessary to us. We'll have to find another way." He added in a gentler voice, "Linne is clever. She might get herself away."

"The Coordinator won't give her the chance," Ryne said. "He knows the value of what he has. He'll keep her in detention."

Weir stopped, swinging around to face Ryne. "Don't you make us do that to you. Don't get any ideas of trying to get her away all by yourself. We're too close to success. Let us think about it."

"She isn't your—your woman," Ryne said angrily.

"She's my niece," Weir said. "She and I are the only family each other has left." He turned and started along the tunnel again. "Just give me your word."

"You have it," Ryne said, and plodded along after him.

XIII

They discussed their problems late that night, and the next day Tara rode to talk with Amso. When she returned, she reported, "Amso will come in the morning to show us the way."

"Then I suppose he'll slip out some night and move everything again," Laszlo said sourly. He looked tired and yet more keyed-up than usual.

"The machine is his responsibility," Tara said gently. "But when we need it, he'll let us take it."

The remainder of the day was a long one, with Ryne finding himself unable to concentrate on his study of the ancient language. The talk centered mostly around the problem of Linne; and Ryne was conscious of the watchfulness in the other's language.

He said finally, "I gave Weir my word. I'm not going to rush out and try to rescue her. Now leave it alone unless you have an idea worth talking about."

Laszlo said curtly, "It isn't our rushing off that concerns me, Ryne. It's what will happen if the Coordinator uses her to force you to go over to his side."

"That's still a long ways off," Ryne said. "First, we have to get the new City built." Pushing at his simmering anger, he looked steadily at Laszlo. "And we have to come up with a way to get the Lowers into that City. To get the Coordinator to open the gates." Rising, he left the room to stand in the darkness on the veranda.

Both moons were shining on the softly rippling sea. But tonight the beauty of it could not cut through Ryne's deep anger. He immersed himself in it, knowing the futility of what he did, yet unable to help himself. Tara had touched his shoulder a second time before he realized that she was beside him.

He turned almost savagely. "I don't want to hear any more about it!"

"I didn't come for that," she said quietly. In the moonlight, her fine, handsome features had an almost ethereal beauty. "I wanted to talk about tomorrow."

"You mean I'm being allowed to go?"

Her touch was light on the back of his hand where it rested on the veranda. "Don't take your anger out on me, Ryne. I'm not Laszlo, nor his alter ego. I'm myself. I do my own thinking, my own judging."

"I'm sorry," he said quickly. "But if he really thinks that I . . ."

"Who knows what Laszlo really thinks?" she demanded. "Now let's forget that. I wanted to tell you about tomorrow. It won't be easy. I didn't tell them in there what Amso said to me today."

He turned, looking down at her and waiting. She said, "He isn't sure that he can find the caves. He went out a few days ago, but he almost lost his way and came back."

"Lost his way! Didn't the man draw a map? Doesn't he have landmarks?"

She laughed suddenly. "What would a City man know about landmarks?"

"I learned in the village," Ryne said. "Don't waste time. What did Amso say?"

"He had landmarks," she admitted. "But during the winter there was a snowslide. And a mud slide too, from the way the mountainsides looked. He knows the general direction, and not much more."

Ryne looked over the sea. Such an easy way out. If he couldn't find a dictionary, he couldn't translate the book. He could pretend, but he knew that with his limited knowledge, it was an impossible task. And sooner or later, Laszlo would have to find another plan. Then he could go back to Upper City, to Linne, to—a failure that was really success.

His hesitation was almost too brief to be noticed. "If Amso'll point us in the right direction and tell us all he can remember, we'll find the cave—and the machine.

And, I hope, a dictionary." He turned to her again. "With all of us hunting, we can't . . ."

"With two of us," she said. "Laszlo has given Weir and Mabton other assignments." She smiled faintly. "I'm only going because Laszlo doesn't think you can manage alone yet." She started away and stopped. "We'll take the wagon and enough food for two days."

"For longer than that," Ryne said, "I'm going to keep looking until I find it."

Strong words, he thought sardonically the next day. With Amso riding his horse alongside, Ryne and Tara jounced along on the wagon seat over ground that grew rougher as they approached the mountains. They had taken a direction Ryne had not followed before, and whenever they came to the top of a rise, he turned to orient himself. He was surprised to see that the great mountainside hiding the City was well behind them and to their right, while the curve of the mountain range had taken them so that Amso's farm was in an almost direct line north and east.

Now they were in the foothills, dropping from crest to valley and climbing back to crest, each one a bit higher than the last. The high peaks beyond were still white with snow, and the small streams they forded rushed with mud-bearing water. The ground of the last few valleys they crossed was still soft from recent thawing. Ryne could feel the change in the air; it had become drier and it held a chill that the air closer to the sea had lost some time before.

The mountains themselves began abruptly, a steeply sloping wall of rock and dirt with a few trees clinging to the lower slopes and then only the rock itself higher up. They stopped with only one narrow valley between them and the mountains.

Amso pulled his horse alongside. "It's somewhere around here," he said. He spoke in the old tongue so that Ryne had to translate for Tara. "There was a stream bed—but the winter changed its course. And on the flat of that mountain ahead, there was a spire. I set my mark by putting the spire right between these two peaks off behind. In the middle of the V. Then straight down, well down where the trees still grow, there was the opening to the cave."

He drew a folded piece of scraped animal skin from his pocket. "Here's the way the route goes inside the mountain."

Ryne looked only briefly at the convoluted map of the caves. His immediate interest was in locating the opening. "You're sure it's that flat ridge ahead?"

"That much I can swear to," Amso said. "But look where the earth slid with spring. The cave itself could be covered with that muck." He stabbed his finger upward. "If the spire was still there, we'd know."

When Ryne had translated, Tara said, "There aren't any other entrances to that warren of caves, Amso?"

"Not a one. It's locked into the mountain as far as I know."

Tara said, "Let's go into the valley and set up our camp."

She lifted the reins and Ryne stopped her. "Wait. Let me look at that ridge from here a minute more."

His eyes swept it—a flat top of unknown depth perhaps a thousand meters in length. On the left end, it dropped off sheer; on the right, it folded into a rising mountain peak, snow-tipped still. In the distance, far behind and much higher than the flat crest, were the twin peaks forming a V. According to Amso there had been a spire of rock thrusting up to center in that V. Apparently the winter's snow had broken the spire and sent it crashing to the ground. Even so, there should be its base and the remnants of the spire itself.

Tomorrow he would climb up there and see. Ryne smiled sourly at himself. First strong words and now a wild idea. He had never climbed anything more precipitous than a duct ladder in his life. And as far as he could tell, there were no rungs on the face of that rocky cliff.

He said to Tara, "All right, let's go down."

They slanted into the valley and pulled through its soft dirt to a stand of trees and bushes that marked the course of the stream. Putting the wagon beneath great spreading branches of one stand of trees, Tara looped the reins and sighed.

"A little shut in, but we have water and firewood close by."

Amso squinted at the slant of the sun. "If I ride hard enough, I can get home in time to do my chores." With a flick at the brim of the broad hat he wore, he trotted away and out of sight.

Ryne said stupidly, "I was counting on his help tomorrow."

"What for? He's told us all he can."

"I thought he could show me how to climb a mountain," Ryne said dryly. He got down from the wagon. "Tell me what to do to set up camp."

She showed him how to stake the horses in a nearby clearing so they could move about on ropes long enough to reach food, water, and shelter and yet not tangle themselves. She had him haul rocks from the stream edge to make a setting for an outdoor fire. "In case the weather lets us stay outside," she explained. And then she had him bring dead branches of downed wood and saw them.

There were quite a few tools in the wagon, Ryne discovered—a saw and an ax, shovels and a pick, long bars flattened at one end, and an immense coil of thin, tough cording. There was also a good supply of food and equipment for sleeping.

By the time they had readied the camp, the slant of the sun had carried it to the tip of the distant mountains. Tara frowned. "The sun is setting red. The natives say that means a storm. In these mountains it could be a strong one."

It was hot in the canyon, with little breeze. And though now the setting of the sun brought some coolness, Ryne was still sweating. Both of them were dirt-stained and, as Tara said, smelled of horses. She found a backwater in the creek and went off with a towel and a change of clothing to disappear behind the screen of bushes along the water. She came back looking fresh.

"Have a bath. It's a little chilly but nice. I'll start our meal."

Ryne took her advice and spent some time splashing in the almost current-free pool. Dressed again, he noticed that the sky was thick with sullen, swelling clouds, and by the time he reached the wagon, the first fat drops of warm rain had started hitting his face and head.

"No fire outside tonight," Tara said. "Have a drink."

She handed Ryne a glass of something golden mixed with water. It was his first experience with Out liquor, and he wasn't sure at first that he liked it. But the warmth radiating through him made the taste more palatable, and soon he grew accustomed to it.

"The Outers make it from a kind of fruit," Tara said. "It's like the brandy we have in the City."

Ryne remembered the brandy. "Only better," he said.

They ate on a small table that unfolded from a side wall, and afterward washed their few dishes. The rain drummed wildly on the roof above them, and now the wind rose to make the tree branches over their heads creak and groan. Ryne thought of the horses, but Tara assured him they would be under shelter by now. They sat and sipped tea, still in restful silence.

A tremendous crack of sound burst on them, making Ryne spill his tea. "Thunder!" Tara said. "Go look out the flap. Maybe you can see your first lightning."

Ryne pulled back the flap and looked out. Wind-spumed rain whipped into his face, and then a flash of light blinded him with its intensity. Brief seconds later the thunder battered his ears and body.

"It's close," Tara said. "I could have made a mistake putting us under the trees."

She explained thunderstorms to Ryne, and by that time the noise was in the distance, only echoing rumbles through the mountains. But the rain continued. They sat awhile longer in companionable silence. Then Tara stirred. "Up early tomorrow," she said. "Let's roll out the beds."

They were in one of the benches along the side wall of the wagon—two thin mattresses with blankets to put over them. Tara said, "You're supposed to sleep under the wagon. But in this kind of weather, you'd float away." With a smile, she unrolled her mattress and his side by side at the rear of the wagon. Spreading the blankets over the mattresses, she turned off the light.

"You stay on the right and I'll take the left."

He could hear her moving and then hear the rustle of

her clothing. He undressed and crawled under his blankets and lay listening to the rain, and then above it he could hear her stirring softly.

"Are you still sure, Ryne?" she asked out of the blackness.

"More sure than ever," Ryne said thinly.

"Because of what the Coordinator did—with your Linne, I mean?"

"That—and everything else I've seen since I've come here." After a moment's silence, he said, "What about you? A High's life should be enough for anyone."

"It's very comfortable," she said. "And it can be very empty. I don't think I've given up as much as you, Ryne. I didn't have anyone up there the way you have your Linne."

He didn't want to talk about Linne or himself, but he said, "I haven't lost her yet."

Again there was silence before she spoke. "Would she think any less of you because we're alone—together this way?"

He didn't understand at first, and then they were together as she moved alongside him. He could feel the smoothness of her skin and the warmth of her breath against his face.

"Do I shock you, Ryne?"

"No," he said. "No." Desperately he clung to the memory and image of Linne; yet soon that ceased to matter, and there was only Tara and the rain softening on the roof above them, and the wind dying slowly away as the storm passed.

XIV

——◦———▶———◦——

The air was fresh and cool after the storm, but the sun bit into Ryne's back as he worked his way up the rock face of the cliff. At first, the climbing was easy, with trees and stubs and outcroppings of rock to hold to. But then the rock became crumbly and there were no more trees.

He found himself on a narrow ledge with nowhere to go but forward. The ground behind him had sharded off and rattled down. He clung to a small projection and looked into the valley. He could see Tara watching, and waiting, and he remembered her last words before letting him start up here.

"Come back in one piece, Ryne. I'd rather spend the night in your arms than putting splints on them."

The thought of her warmed him and he edged along, wondering what he would do when he reached the end of this ledge. It came suddenly, and he found himself staring at a V-shaped groove that slanted upward across the face of what, from below, looked like sheer cliff. He wondered if he could brace his feet in the sides of the groove and claw his way upward.

He could, and at the end of the groove was another going in the opposite direction, and beyond that a third, so that he worked back and forth until he found himself belly down on the flat top of the cliff. His breath gusted in and out. Up here, for all the sunlight, he could feel a chill bathing his sweaty body, and when he crawled to his knees and looked back, the distance he had come frightened him a little. Below, Tara was still visible only because she moved against the still backdrop of the valley

102

floor. He waved and thought he saw her answer. Then, rising, he turned and studied the flat area around him.

It was completely barren except for a scatter of large boulders and, some distance away, the bulk of a massive piece of dark-reddish rock. The color was so distinctive from the dull grays of the surrounding rocks that Ryne went quickly to it. Visible now was a scatter of other stones, many almost cylindrical in cross section, and all of them red, stretching due eastward.

Ryne grunted with the satisfaction of having guessed right. This scatter of stones was the remains of Amso's spire; sometime during the winter, a heavy burden of snow or a strong wind had found its weak spot and sent it tumbling from its base. Pacing it, he decided that it had once risen a full ten meters from the two-meter-high stub remaining.

He climbed to the top of one of the stubs and turned until he could see the notch in the distant mountains. He maneuvered his body until he was sighting dead center in the V of the notch. Stooping carefully, he made a line, using loose bits of rubble, that angled slightly across the top of the stub. Then he turned and looked for Tara. She was nowhere in sight, and so he sought some landmarks he could use once he was back on the ground.

He located a tree whose top rose well above those surrounding it. He judged the stand of trees to be on a ridge a good hundred meters from their camp. When he stood astraddle his line of rubble, his eyes were directly on the tree, his back squarely fitted into the notch in the distant mountains.

It would have to do, Ryne decided. Climbing down from the stub of rock, he considered a way to return to the camp. Going down the way he had come was too dangerous, he realized. He explored the flat; at the far-western edge on the side opposite their camp, he discovered a comparatively easy slope leading down to the flatland. He started the descent, and by the time the sun was sliding past its zenith, he was once more on level ground. Now he had only to make the long journey around the great flat-topped cliff and he should be back in the valley they had chosen for their camp.

It was early evening when Ryne limped into view of the

wagon. Tara came running toward him, her hands out-stretched. "I was about to start out after you! Whatever happened?"

Ryne felt her full, firm body in his, and for all of his weariness he felt a stir of hunger. She tilted up her head and he kissed her gently. "Let me have a bath and I'll tell you all about it. And something to eat. I missed my lunch."

An hour later, a glass of Out liquor warming him, Ryne wolfed at the meal Tara had prepared. She listened to his description of what he had found. "I hunted all over the hillside. I can't find a cave opening anywhere," she said.

"There has to be one," Ryne said. "It's probably under the dirt that Amso said slid during the spring."

She made a face. "Have you ever done any digging with a shovel?"

"No."

"Tomorrow, you'll think today's jaunt was a stroll over the meadow," she said.

Ryne was a little surprised when he found that Tara was right. By midday, he had dug a dozen test holes along the imaginary line between his tree and the notch in the mountains. He retreated to the wagon for a noon meal, his hands sore and threatening to blister.

Tara found some gloves, and the afternoon was a little easier. Even so, he found himself working more slowly, found each shovelful of the heavy, moist dirt heavier. It was past sunset when he plunged his shovel into the dirt and found himself sprawling face down, the shovel gone from his hand.

Ryne rolled to his feet. Tara was digging below him and a few meters to one side. "I found something!"

Together they cleared away the loose dirt to reveal a cave mouth. Ryne's shovel lay just out of reach on the stony floor of a natural cave.

"This has to be the one!"

"My guess too," Ryne agreed. "Tomorrow we'll take the lamps and the rope and have a look." He grinned at her through a mask of dirt-caked sweat. "Tonight, I just want a bath, a drink, a meal, and . . ." He stopped, discon-certed at the strength of the rush of desire for her that swept through him.

She kissed him, dirt and all. "First things first," she said. "Let's get back to camp."

They found the dictionaries within an hour after they entered the cave the next morning. Amso had carried his trust only past the first turn. Here the high-roofed natural-stone tunnel widened to a vault. In it were two tall files filled with micro-cards and labeled, as nearly as Ryne could make out, "Personnel Files" and "Ship's Log." Beyond them were stacked some twenty plastic boxes of various sizes. Most seemed to be spare parts for the machine. Finally came the wheeled box in which the machine sat. It was surprisingly small compared to Ryne's expectations.

He found the dictionaries in one of the cartons, beneath a ten-volume set of the encyclopedia of which Laszlo had one part. There were three volumes, labeled "Scientific and Technical Dictionary," although he was not certain of the word 'Technical' until he looked it up in Volume 3.

They returned with a feeling of a kind of triumph, the carton of encyclopedias and the dictionaries riding in the wagon. As they swung into the yard where Laszlo and Weir stood watching them, they burst spontaneously into a song that had been popular in the City two years before.

Tara leaped from the wagon before Ryne brought it to a halt. She smiled at Laszlo. "Success! We found it. Ryne found it!"

Laszlo said only, "Good. Let's get to work." He turned and went into the house. Ryne came down from the wagon seat and touched Tara as if to absorb some of the disappointment etched on her features.

Weir said, "Last night we got word that the Bully Boys are raiding some of our group leaders and their lieutenants. Somebody leaked information about who they were. Already five men have been badly beaten." He added sourly, "The Wardens are deploring it, of course, but they don't seem to be able to be in the right place at the right time to stop it."

"At least Laszlo can't say Ryne had anything to do with it," Tara cried. "He's been with one of us since you took him to that meeting."

"Even then, I couldn't give you the names of over three of those men," Ryne said.

"Tell that to Laszlo," Weir said. "He thinks Ryne has some kind of transmitter—or maybe he believes in magic." His voice was heavy and tired.

Ryne swung away from them and went into the house. He found the big parlor empty, and he went to Laszlo's door. Without knocking, he jerked it open and stepped inside. Laszlo was at his desk. His glance was cold and still as he looked up at Ryne.

"You're going to have to make up your mind one way or the other," Ryne said bluntly. "Either you trust me or you don't. If you do, then get all this garbage out of your mind. If you don't, say so, and I'll go back to Upper City and we can forget I was ever here."

Laszlo's lips rimmed with white. "You talk to me that way! I make the mandates here, not you!"

Ryne said softly, "As Tara pointed out, I had no opportunity to name those men—I don't even know who they are."

"We have a list. You could have stolen it long enough to make a copy."

"And when would I have got that information to the Coordinator?"

"You could have found a way."

Ryne put his hands on Laszlo's table and bent forward, his face inches from Laszlo's. "You," he said, "are a damned paranoid. I don't think you're fit to lead the Lowers out of the Old City."

Laszlo stood up abruptly, his chair scraping back and clattering to the floor. His face was a sickly white, his eyes shattered shards of ice. Behind him, Weir said, "I'm beginning to agree with Ryne. Now that he has the dictionary, we can build the new City. Among us, there are technicians enough. I'm not sure we need you any longer, Laszlo."

Laszlo stared at him, and then he sat down, slumping so that his head hung almost to his knees. He remained that way, his body shaking from the violence of his breathing.

Weir called, "Tara, Laszlo's gone into shock again." He turned to Ryne. "Help me get him to bed."

When they lifted Laszlo, the sight of his features stunned Ryne. They were dulled, slack, without the character he had come to think of as the essence of the man. Carefully, he helped Weir put the surprisingly light body on the cot.

"How long will he be like this?"

Weir shrugged. "I had to do it to him about six months ago when he convinced himself both Mabton and I were selling ourselves to the Coordinator. He came around completely in a week that time."

Tara came in carrying a small case. Opening it, she took out a pressure injector, bared Laszlo's arm, and tapped the activator. He jerked slightly and then began breathing less gustily. In a short while he was asleep.

"Isn't there some other way . . ." Ryne began.

"Not with Laszlo," Tara said. "Between overwork and his—his paranoia, there just isn't any other way. He'll be all right when he's rested." She nodded to Weir. "It shouldn't be as long. He looks much better than he did the other time. Maybe only three or four days."

Ryne's euphoria at having found the dictionaries was completely gone. But he said, "In that case I'll get to work. Maybe having a translation ready when he does come around will help."

When he was gone, Weir shook his head at Tara. "I wish I knew exactly where Ryne stood. Until the Coordinator let him know he had Linne, I would have trusted Ryne all the way. Now I'm not so sure."

"I am," Tara said defensively. "How could he have learned the names of the group leaders and the lieutenants?"

"I was in the doorway, and I heard Laszlo as much as accuse him of stealing our master list of names," Weir said. "And Ryne has been working in here a lot. He could have copied that list."

"Even if he did, how could he have sent the information to the Coordinator? How and when?"

Weir said with faint amusement, "Laszlo thinks he has a secret transmitter stashed somewhere." He chuckled. "That answered the 'how,' I guess, but it still doesn't account for the 'when.' He's been in constant sight of one or another of us since we came from the meeting."

Tara nodded. "Of course. "He and I . . ." She broke off, pressing a hand to her mouth. "Oh, no!"

Weir's smile disappeared. Tara said miserably, "Yesterday morning, Ryne climbed a cliff to take a sighting. He said he had to get down by going in another direction and walk all the way around the cliff. He didn't reach camp until almost dark."

Weir let out a gusty breath. "I'm glad Laszlo didn't hear that. It would put him in permanent shock." He started from the room. "I think we'd better take turns with Ryne. One of us should be with him whenever he decides to go out for some fresh air."

XV

In the middle of his first night working on the translation, Ryne made a discovery—virtually all of the scientific and technical words he had to look up were constructed from a small group of root words. Once he recognized this characteristic of the language, he was able to move more swiftly than he had hoped.

He had already reached the point where he could think in the ancient tongue as he read it, his understanding interrupted only by those long, unfamiliar words. But now he was able to take them apart and understand them, and in a short while he found he could "feel" their meaning as part of the total context.

By the night of the third day, he had read twice through the section in the encyclopedia on the use of the city-building machine and he felt ready to make a written translation. Tara found him with his head slumped on the desk top, one hand reaching out for the writing instrument. He was asleep.

Her touch awakened him. "You damn fool. Do you want to end up in bed like Laszlo? Go get some sleep. You haven't had over two hours a night since we got back."

She had a cup of tea for him and he sipped it gratefully. "I'm fine," he said. "Now that I've learned the way the language is put together, reading it is no trick at all." He gulped more tea. "How is Laszlo?"

"Not as good as we'd hoped. He'll need another three or four days."

"I'm about ready," Ryne said. "If we had to, we could

start the machine working tomorrow. Isn't there any way of hurrying Laszlo's recovery? He still has to work out a final plan to . . ."

"No," she said. "No, we can't hurry him. And no, he doesn't have to work out a plan. Weir told me that he solved the problem while we were gone." She stopped speaking.

Ryne's eyebrows went up. "Meaning, I'm not supposed to know what it is?"

"No," she said, "you're not supposed to know what it is. But I can tell you this much. It's a good plan. And Weir and Mabton and Corso will go to the City to start it working as soon as the new City is built."

Ryne said, "Does it consider Linne . . ." He broke off. "That's why I'm not being told, isn't it? Because they're afraid I might wreck it trying to help her?"

Tara nodded. Ryne said, "It makes sense—from their point of view. But I don't know myself what I might do." He looked carefully into Tara's face and dropped his words slowly. "Maybe I won't do anything. Maybe it doesn't matter that much any more."

She caught his arm. "Ryne, you have to do something! You can't just let her rot there." Her eyes were pleading. "Do you mean because of us, there at the camp, that you'd forget . . ."

"No," he said. "I'm not forgetting. I just meant that maybe the Coordinator doesn't have the same hold on me as he did before. Maybe we can get Linne out after everything is over."

He thought he saw fear and shock in Tara's eyes, but she turned away too quickly for him to be sure. She said only, "Please get some rest," as she left the room.

Ryne returned to the table where his work lay spread out. He knuckle-rubbed his eyes and yawned. He was too keyed up to rest; too many ideas were pounding through his mind. Perhaps it was the lack of sleep; perhaps he had caught some of Laszlo's disease. But he was frightened.

He slept—head on the table as before—and then he wakened to reread the material and to begin writing it in the current tongue in his easily readable handscript. Writing it, finding just the right words and translating the subtleties of ideas, took a lot longer than he had expected. He had barely dented the first page of fine print when it was dinnertime.

Mabton was there, fresh from a trip to the City, a wide smile on his usually sour face. His conversation monopolized the table talk. And, Ryne admitted, he had a right to smile. The night before he had taken a backpack full of the sticks of explosive powder the Farm used for blasting free tree trunks. These he carried to town and showed the group leaders and lieutenants how to light the fuses and how long to hold the sticks before throwing them. Their first efforts had blown a meter-wide hole in the paving directly in front of a gang of charging Bully Boys. Across Lower City, another group leader had promptly stopped an attack when his explosive stick blew a cornice from a building, and a piece of ricocheting material had killed one of the Bully Boys. An angry attack from Warden vehicles had ended with one of them upside down, its bottom shattered, and Wardens running or driving off as fast as they could.

"The Coordinator declared a temporary truce," Mabton said. "It doesn't rest easy, and I suspect the Auxiliaries are being mobilized. But for the moment, anyway, Lower City isn't being terrified out of cooperating with us." He added almost casually, "The explosives were Laszlo's idea."

Ryne saw now the basis of Laszlo's plan. He said, "If we wait too long to get the new City built, we won't stand a chance of getting the Lowers to it. I know the Coordinator's way of thinking. He won't just be organizing his Auxiliaries, he'll be preparing a defense against explosives."

His answer was a startled silence. Into it, Tara said, "Nobody told Ryne about the plan." Still none of them spoke. She added defensively, "What Ryne is trying to tell you is that he's read the instructions. He knows how to make the machine work now."

Mabton shook his head. "The Coordinator still has Linne."

Whatever his full meaning might be, only Weir seemed to understand. He said, "That's right. We'll have to wait for Laszlo to come around before we do anything. This is his show."

Ryne scraped back his chair. "Why don't you lock me up and get me off your minds?" He glared angrily around the table. "Don't you think I know that someone's always been posted at the door of the room where I work? That I know there's someone trailing me whenever I go out for air?"

"Take it easy," Weir said. "Try and look at it from our position."

"Maybe I can dream that vision up," Ryne said. He went to the bunkroom and lay down, removing only his boots. The surge of anger had drained even more from him and he fell into a thick sleep.

He had set his mental alarm for five hours of rest, and within minutes of the time limit, he was sitting up in the late-night darkness. He could hear soft breathing in the room and he rose quietly. He slipped into the parlor and from there to the door of Laszlo's room. A light burned as it always did, and when he looked in, he saw Laszlo's figure on the cot humped under a blanket. He moved on to the door of Tara's room. His hand trembled a little as he reached for the latch, wondering what she would think if she should awaken and see him looking in at her.

With an effort, he rejected the hunger clawing at him and turned away. His light footfalls carried him to the veranda. The swift-racing hither moon was alone in the sky, silvering a mirror-like sea. The air was pleasantly cool and the night was utterly still.

The fear Ryne had felt yesterday afternoon flooded back over him. He stood with his hands on the railing of the veranda, staring unseeingly outward and trying to pin down the cause of that fright.

Mostly it centered on Linne—Linne and Laszlo. Because he knew that once awake, Laszlo would demand the translated instructions. Linne would not be a concern of his as she was to Weir, to Ryne, and—apparently—to Tara. If he saw a chance of success, now that his final plan was made, he would drive ahead, letting nothing nor anyone stand in his way.

Ryne smiled grimly as a thought occurred to him. What if Amso should have moved the machine by now, or moved it before Laszlo could get to it? No, that was impossible. It was one thing he had no need to worry about. The great dirt slide of the spring had left too much soft soil at too steep a pitch for Amso to take a wagon or even horses into the caves. The only way the machine could be moved now was to make it go under its own power. And only Ryne knew how to do that.

The idea caught hold of him. It grew as the moonlight with the rise of the nether moon. What if he went now, if he built the new City? Then he could go to the old City and find a way to free Linne, find a way to stop the Coordinator long enough for Laszlo's plan to go into operation. If he was clever enough to get away from his watchdogs, he could do it. After reading the encyclopedia, he understood some things about the City that none of the others knew. Things that would give him an edge on the Coordinator— once Linne was safe.

Ryne glanced around in the stillness. If anyone was awake to watch him, they were being more clever about it than they had been before. He could hear only night sounds, see only moon shadows. Quickly, he stepped from the veranda and padded around the house to the barn. Again he stopped, and again he heard no movement from the direction of the house.

He slipped into the dark barn and used the thin trickle of moonlight coming through a high window to find his way to his horse. He stopped suddenly, one stall short of his own. The horse that should have been there was missing. To make sure, he eased into the stall and felt around through the darkness. There was only the bed of hay; horse, saddle, and bridle were gone.

The implication of the missing horse hurried Ryne's movements. He risked a little noise now, moving along to his own horse and saddling it quickly. He led the horse out and to the rear of the barn before he mounted. He walked it over the thickening grass until he reached the first low hill. From its crest he looked back. The farm remained dark and silent. He nodded, sure that they would not have expected him to wake so soon.

He forced from his mind the meaning of the missing horse. He was too busy riding at a speed faster than he had ever risked before. He clung unashamedly to the leather as he urged the horse in a direct line to the base of the bluff that held the cave with the machine.

For a time he could move swiftly over moonlit trails. Then the forest closed in and he had to slow down, picking his way through darkness. Finally daylight broke and he was able to pick up speed again. Even so, the sun had risen before Ryne sighted the great sprawl of dirt and the small, dark opening marking the cave mouth.

He might be too late after all. A horse was staked in the nearest meadow, and the soft dirt showed the recent marks of someone climbing up to the cave. Ryne moved his horse to another, smaller meadow, and then went on foot to the base of the earth slide. He climbed slowly, working along the far edge until he was almost level with the cave mouth. Then he moved across the soft dirt. He stopped at the opening, holding his breath as he listened for sounds from inside.

He could hear nothing, and so he eased himself quickly inside. He took off his boots and padded over the cold stone in his stocking feet, carrying the boots in his left hand and feeling along the wall with his right as the outside light grew fainter with distance.

He swore at himself for not having thought to bring a torch. The darkness became total as he rounded the bend. The vault should lie just ahead, as he remembered, and again he stopped, stilling his breath.

He could hear sounds now, and suddenly a hand torch flashed its beam in his direction. Ryne saw its first flicker and drew quickly back around the corner of the tunnel. He heard a grunt. The light remained on, so that he realized he had been heard approaching, and a trap was set for him with the darkness. But the trap had been sprung and had caught nothing. Maybe the person in there would dismiss the sounds he had heard. Ryne hoped so. He would need that advantage.

Carefully he eased his head around the corner. The torch had been laid on one of the boxes, its beam aimed at the near side of the machine. Amso crouched down, bending forward as if putting something under the big box that housed the machine. Ryne frowned, wondering what the man could be doing. Then he saw a match flare up, saw the sputter of flame as a wick caught fire. The fool! He was trying to blow up the machine with explosive powder.

Ryne drew out of sight and listened as Amso scrambled to get his torch and then run for the front of the cave. The torchlight flashed at the corner and then Amso was within reach of Ryne. Amso went sprawling over an outstretched foot. The vicious chop of Ryne's fist against the back of his neck coincided with the battering, blinding explosion of the powder. Ryne crouched over the motionless body, blinking the glare out of his eyes and shaking his head to relieve the pressure that had beaten against his eardrums.

Somewhere in the far reaches of the cave, an opening was creating a draft that sucked the smoke and the powder smell from the vault. Within a few minutes, Ryne was able to take Amso's torch and go up to the machine. He had expected what he saw, but even so he laughed with relief. The explosive powder had done nothing to the machine but streak the side of the housing a sooty black.

Ryne went to the other side of the machine and stood repeating to himself the instructions he had filled his mind with. His hand reached out for a small protuberance and pressed. A door slid aside, making room enough for him to crawl inside.

He was in what the encyclopedia called the control room. He sat in the single chair and studied the instrument panel in front of him. Each of the numerous switches was labeled, as were the dials above some of them. To one side was the keyboard for programming the machine's computer, and between Ryne's chair and the control panel were two footpedals with a lever just to their right. On the panel itself, extending toward Ryne on a long arm, was a small wheel.

Ryne read the labels on the switches until he found the one he wanted. He depressed it and the control room filled with soft light. With a prayer that centuries of disuse and innumerable trips behind teams of horses from one cave to another had not disabled the machine, Ryne pushed in a second switch.

Beneath him he could feel a faint throbbing start up. He began to depress one switch after another. The front of the protective housing rolled up to let him see out. Great lights beat against the outer darkness, illuminating the vault completely. Tentatively, Ryne pushed the lever forward and touched his right foot to one of the pedals. The machine moved without hesitation, rolling gently forward on its great wheels. Ryne experimented with using the small wheel to turn the machine, the left pedal to stop it, and the right pedal to increase its speed. He found that with the lever forward, he would move forward; with it back, he would move backward.

Finally he felt ready. Aiming the machine for the tunnel, he eased it slowly forward. Halfway around the corner he stopped, climbed out, and picked up Amso's still-motionless body. Moving it back into the vault, he turned off the torch and put it in one of Amso's hands, and then returned to the machine. He negotiated the corner and started down the corridor. He found that he had to steer absolutely straight or the housing scraped against the rough stone walls. Finally he saw the daylight ahead, and then he was at the cave mouth. Turning off the outside lights, he studied the steep pitch of soft dirt that led to the valley floor. Whether the big machine could fight through that dirt and remain upright and in motion he had no way of knowing.

"The book claims it can go through anything," Ryne said aloud. Releasing the pedal that held the machine motionless, he started it gently forward. The front dipped. The forward wheels struck soft dirt. Ryne felt a pitching and a sharp swaying. But some inner mechanism apparently brought it quickly back to an upright position.

The descent was agonizing in its slowness. Twice the machine found very soft dirt and tilted dangerously. But each time it righted itself and dug its way toward the valley.

Once at the bottom, Ryne opened the door and climbed out to look back at the cave. He could see Amso, stumbling and staggering through the soft dirt, running to reach Ryne.

Back inside, Ryne started the machine moving over the trail he and Tara had originally come here on. He increased the speed as he became more and more adept at steering the great, clumsy-looking box. Twice he had to spin the wheel frantically as the road bent without warning, but finally he broke into the open, climbed a hill, and dropped into the valley where the new City was to be built.

The old City lay just to Ryne's right, beyond the great rise of hill looming to the east. At night, he would be able to see its glow; now the brightness of the slanting sun and the hill hid it completely. Ryne moved the machine to the center of the valley, turning it so that when it had built its City, the gates would be facing eastward. Then he sat quietly, thinking of the instructions for making the machine do its primary function—the creation of an entire City, functioning and ready for me to live in.

Laszlo had never told Ryne what kind of City he envisioned. The machine was preprogrammed to build a stock, conventional City of one level spread over an area of 60 square kilometers. A City complete with factories for making synthetic foods, clothing—whatever necessities men might need; complete with buildings for living, for business, for government; and complete with drains and ducts and a great central core running to tap power far down in the earth.

Changes and innovations could be programmed into the building of a City, but Ryne wasted no time considering any. He set the machine for its standard program, rearranging only a few of the steps so that the protective force dome would be created first, and that the dome would remain sealed until the machine had finished its work. Then it was to slide open the gates. Finally, he gave the machine instructions to wait twenty minutes before starting to work. Then he jumped out and hurried across the valley floor to the hill. Climbing to a point beyond the area the force field would enclose, he sat down to rest and to watch.

Ryne's wrist chrono said that the twenty minutes had passed. Yet as far as he could tell, the machine remained silent, immobile. Then he saw it tremble. The sides of the box folded up to form a kind of canopy. Great arms swept out from the formerly hidden body of the machine. The hum of its powerful atomic motors throbbed on the air. Ryne could not see the force dome as it was being built, being woven from the very stuff of the air around him; yet he knew this was happening.

Slowly, a translucence grew between Ryne and the machine until he could make it out only dimly. But he knew what it was doing. With the force dome finished, it would now be busily boring a great core into the earth. And from the dirt of that core, the machine would weave the building materials it needed, the piping and the wiring, the walls and the roofs, the streets—all of the City.

And it would do everything between now and the time the sun rose again in the morning. Ryne got to his feet. He could do no more here, and he had a long walk back to where he had left his horse. If he hurried, he might get to the meadow before darkness came.

He was at the crest of the hill when he saw Amso coming on his horse. He rode almost into Ryne, jerking his horse aside at the last instant. His face was twisted in wild anger.

"Stop it!" he cried. "Stop it, man!"

"It's too late," Ryne said. "I couldn't get it to stop if I wanted to. And I don't want to."

Amso said thickly, "You crazy City fool! You've just damned those Lowers to a worse life than they're living now!"

XVI

Ryne had no clear memory of the next moments. He remembered only the harsh violence of contact with another body, the neigh of a frightened horse, and himself tumbling down the hillslope toward the translucent dome, Amso tangled up with him.

Amso was a powerful man, but Ryne was the younger and stronger. When they rolled to a stop he swung above Amso, pinning him to the ground with a knee in his chest and holding both strong wrists in one hand.

"Now," Ryne said softly, "I want to know what you meant by my damning the Lowers. I want to know why you tried to destroy the machine."

Amso rolled his head back and forth in negation. "You're crazy," he cried. "You get off me and stop that thing!"

"I can't," Ryne said. "The dome is solid until the machine finishes its work. Then it will open the gates—for the Lowers."

Amso made a futile effort to buck free, but Ryne's weight and strength were too great. He sagged back panting. "There won't be no Lowers come to your City." His eyes gleamed wildly. "No damn Lowers to ruin the Out. None of your City scum to take away the clean, free land here!"

Shock and surprise flooded through Ryne. He hadn't realized that the Outers had carried within them the seeds of hatred so long. How many years back had there been the last battle between Outers and City people? Not years, but centuries.

119

Ryne shook himself free of Amso's dislike. "You can't stop them, Amso. No one man can stop them."

Amso's face twisted in a grin of triumph. "The Coordinator can," he said. "When he learns what Laszlo's fool plan is, he'll stop it. Explosive powder! He'll have a defense against that in no time."

His eyes took on wildness again. "You know what he'll do, Ryne? He'll fool your Lowers. He'll fool Weir and Corso and Mabton when they go to the City to start the Lowers off to the gates. He'll make them think everything is going their way. He'll let every one of those renegade Lowers crawl out of their holes. Then he'll move in the Wardens and the Auxiliaries—surround the Lowers. And they'll have defenses against the powder. Hell, it can blow a stump but it's no good against anything tough—like that machine box."

Ryne had to agree. Even a weak force field would stop the destructive force of the powder, and if not by now, then soon, the Coordinator would see to it that every Auxiliary and every Warden was equipped with some kind of simple protective device—a field or a more elemental barrier, a shield.

He said aloud, "If you don't want Laszlo to succeed, why did you show him the machine? Why did you help the Lowers who came to the Out as refugees?"

"I didn't know what they had in mind when they first came," Amso said. "And Laszlo fooled me with all his fancy talk. He didn't tell me what he was going to do until it was nigh too late."

"That's not true," Ryne said. "You mean you weren't talked into being afraid of Lowers in the new City until recently—by your friend from the Farm. The friend who told you that I already knew how to make the machine work. That's why you went last night to destroy it. You thought you had plenty of time, until you were told otherwise."

He asked curiously, "How long have you kept the Coordinator posted on everything that happens here?"

"You're crazy. I never saw the Coordinator in my life."

"No, but you've been told about him. You know a lot about the City, Amso. You've been told a lot about it." Ryne squeezed his hand down on Amso's wrists. "What do you use, Amso—a wireless transmitter and receiver with pickup amplifiers every half-kilometer or so? And then a carrier wire running into the City? A direct line to the Coordinator?"

Amso's expression tried to reject Ryne's words, but his eyes gave him away. Ryne nodded. It was the only logical explanation. Amso would have a communication station somewhere—probably in his barn. Messages about the activities and plans at the Farm would be given to him, and he would send them to the Coordinator, receiving instructions in return. And the only possible way he could reach the Coordinator would be by the technique Ryne had described—a wireless communicator with amplifiers every so often to pick up and increase the signal and send it on to the next station. But at the edge of the City, at the Dome, the signal would have to go through one of the tunnels by wire and on into the ducts and up to the Coordinator.

It was not something that had just been thrown together. It was too sophisticated a system for even an Outer as clever as Amso to have devised for himself. Somehow it must have been brought into the Out, piece by piece, part by part, over a period of time, and Amso trained to use it.

Ryne wanted more information, and he tried the shock technique to bring Amso's anger back to loosen his tongue. "Even if you're right and the Coordinator stops the Lowers, it won't be for long," Ryne said. "There'll always be more of them—and more of us. Laszlo has outsmarted the Coordinator up to now. He can do it again."

Amso laughed at him. "Outsmarted! Hell, man, the Coordinator knew every move Laszlo was going to make before he made it. You think he couldn't have stopped all this before now? He could—any time. But he wanted to get Laszlo men where they wouldn't cause no more trouble. And he wanted to get Laszlo where nobody'd listen to him any more. And that's what'll happen after the Lowers find themselves worse off than they've ever been. And with Weir and Mabton and Corso caught, what can Laszlo do?"

The whole pattern of events fell into place in Ryne's mind. He had been duped, manipulated from the beginning, he and Linne both. The thought of Linne wrenched at him inside. Fear for her struck at him so that, unaware, he slacked off his grip against Amso. He felt the powerful surge of the body under him, and he tried to regain his advantage. He was too late. Amso rolled free, leaped to his feet, and kicked out. Ryne caught the toe of Amso's heavy boot on his temple, and he slumped backward, only half conscious that Amso was running up the hill, calling to his horse.

When Ryne was able to navigate without having to stop and be sick from dizziness, darkness had come. The night was a chill one, and dark until the hither moon rose and began its gambol across the sky. He trudged toward the distant valley where his own horse was staked. Twice he stopped and looked back, and each time the sight of the new City glowing against the night made him turn and hurry onward.

He thought of those back at the Farm. They couldn't avoid seeing the great, new glow in the sky. They would know what it meant, what he had done. And without waiting for Laszlo to get well, they would do what had to be done. They would go into the City and start the plan working. They would go into a trap that condemned them to living deaths.

Ryne stopped to rest, the dizziness from Amso's kick striking him again. He could have gone the other way, to the tunnel, and tried to stop Weir and the others from going into the City. But would they have listened to him? He had built the City in defiance of Weir's insistence that they wait for Laszlo to recover. And he still had no plan for getting Linne free.

He realized that even if he could count on their listening to him, he was too far from the Farm or the old City now. His horse should be just over the next rise, if he could find the strength to go that far.

He climbed to his feet and plodded on, fighting the urge to hurry, conserving what strength remained to him. When he found the horse, he released it from the staked line and hauled himself into the saddle. He started the horse back the way he had come.

After a time the nether moon arose, and together the two moons made a fine, clear light. The night grew chill, arousing Ryne to wakefulness. He realized suddenly that for a time he had ridden in semi-consciousness, and he discovered that the horse was going not to the Farm but directly to Amso's place. He sat up straighter and tried to puzzle out his own reasoning.

Amso's own words echoed in his mind: " 'The Coordinator can. When he learns what Laszlo's fool plan is . . .' "

And that was the key. Amso had not taken the time to pass the information of the plan on to the Coordinator. He must have received it at the same time that he received the information about Ryne's knowing how to work the machine. And he had left immediately to destroy the machine, thinking that the more important job.

Eagerly Ryne sent the horse hurrying forward. Then he swore at himself. Amso had escaped from him before dark. Long before now he would have reached home and transmitted his message. The most Ryne could do by going to his ranch would be to destroy his communicator— if it could be found.

That wouldn't be necessary. All he needed to do was find a single pickup amplifier. A break in the system would make it as worthless as smashing the communicator itself.

Ryne drew the horse to a stop. He sat on a hillcrest, looking down at the dark barn and dimly lighted house that marked Amso's place. Mentally, he drew a line between here and the hill where the tunnels leading into the old City began. A direct line would pass almost through the Farm. Then it would have to be an elbow. Again Ryne drew a mental map of the territory. A line running so that it would pass to the west of the Farm by a half kilometer or so followed closely the clumps of trees scattered only sparsely across the open land. Logically, it would be in trees that the pickup amplifiers would be hidden.

Ryne turned from Amso's lights and headed along the line he thought the communications would follow. He stopped at the first trees he came to and studied them. Only then did he realize the hopelessness of finding anything as small as a pickup amplifier.

Swearing at himself for having a thick head and at Amso for kicking him in that thick head, he started for the Farm. Once more he stopped. Again he was charging full tilt without thinking the problem through. Going to the Farm might well get him locked up, restrained.

His first problem was to somehow stop Weir and the others from going into the City and starting the Lowers toward the gates. His second problem was to get Linne free. Only then would there be any chance of negotiating with the Coordinator.

Ryne rode forward, but more slowly. He came to the Farm well behind it and studied the dark outbuildings and the lighted house. Carefully he rode forward, keeping the barn between himself and the house. At the rear of the barn, he stopped, tied the tired horse, and started forward on foot. He stopped at the corner of the barn to look in the direction of the Cities. As he had thought, the glow of the new City was a great beacon against the night. Someone here must have seen it shortly after dark.

Ryne was not surprised then to discover three horses missing from the stalls. Weir and the others would have gone as soon as they realized the meaning of the new light in the sky. Tara's horse was gone too, and Ryne walked to the rear door and went inside.

He found Laszlo sitting up, his eyes clear. He was close to the fire, a blanket wrapped around his shoulders. He looked in silence at Ryne. Then he said, "You started the machine."

"Yes," Ryne said. "The City will be finished by morning. Then the gates will open."

"Why?" Laszlo demanded. "Why didn't you wait for me? What did you and the Coordinator gain?"

"He gained nothing," Ryne said. He sat down, aware suddenly of the implication behind his building the City so soon. Once Laszlo heard of the trap waiting for the Lowers, for Weir and Mabton and Corso, he would assume Ryne had built the City early just for the purpose of trapping them. But there was no choice except to tell him what had happened.

"I'm not the one who's been feeding the Coordinator information about your plans," Ryne said. "He's known all along what you've been doing, what you were going to do. He knew about your plan to get me here. He knew about Linne. He knew about the jamming of the scan before it happened. He knew because Amso told him."

Disbelief lay heavy in Laszlo's eyes. Quickly, Ryne told him what had happened near the new City. Laszlo shook his head. "Impossible. How could a—a farmer like Amso build a communicator—a wireless communicator at that?"

"Amso didn't build it," Ryne said. "It was brought here and he was taught to use it." He appeared to shift the subject abruptly. "When did Tara leave?"

"Weir saw the glow of the new City and he and the others left almost at once. Tara was cleaning the kitchen. She finished her work and then went to Amso's for some cream."

Ryne said, "Tara uses a lot of cream." He got to his feet. "How long have the men been gone?"

Laszlo smiled at him. "Over two hours. You haven't a chance of catching them, Ryne."

"No," Ryne admitted. "But maybe I can stop them before they get all the Lowers moving into the Coordinator's trap."

He could see that Laszlo believed nothing he had said. There was a barrier between them, a barrier separating their minds as thoroughly as a force dome separated a City from its surroundings. He said only, "I'm going to get Linne. When Tara comes back, tell her that."

Rising, he started away, and stopped. "Tell her too that she'd be wasting her time riding back to Amso. I'm going to find the communication line and cut it. As soon as I get to the tunnel leading to the City, there won't be any more contact with the Coordinator."

Laszlo seemed to pay no attention to Ryne's last statement. He said, "You're going to trade my men for your Linne?"

"No," Ryne said, "there'll be no trades. I'm going to try to get her out and your men too—and the Lowers as well."

"Making sure you save your own hide," Laszlo said savagely.

"That too," Ryne said. "Along with yours."

XVII

—◆—◆—◆—

Finding the communication line was not difficult once Ryne decided to search the tunnel itself. It was a fine wire laid in the joint between the rough tunnel floor and the equally rough stone wall. Dirt had been sifted over it to cut down the chance of a torch picking up the almost invisible sheen of the insulation. Ryne cut a ten-meter length from the line, rolled it up, and put it in the bag he carried.

He had taken only the time to fill a saddlebag before leaving the Farm. Laszlo had made no effort to stop him; either he was too weak to move or he discounted Ryne's ability to do anything. Without hindrance, Ryne had stowed in the saddlebag a pair of wire cutters, as many sticks of the explosive powder, each fused, as he found room for, and a long coil of extra wick. He wanted one more item, but there was none available at the Farm. He spent a good deal of his time on the ride to the City considering where he might find a remote communicator.

The plan he had sought, and had lacked the clearness of thought for, came clearly and sharply to him as he talked to Laszlo. He realized its weaknesses as well as its strengths; just as he realized that the penalty for failure was more than continued suspicion of himself. It would not even be Exile, not any longer. It would be permanent detention in the gloomy cells of Warden Central. It would be an existence to make death welcome when it came.

Ryne had no illusions about the Coordinator, not any longer. A man who could prepare as carefully as he had, who could manipulate lives as he had manipulated Ryne's and Linne's and the others'—that man would not hesitate to take the final step to provide himself and his precious City with permanent protection. That he had acted and would act in what he considered the best interests of the society he was responsible for changed nothing. Whatever the Coordinator's motivation, the Lowers would be just as repressed, those involved in the revolt just as thoroughly imprisoned. Their lives would be made no easier by knowing that the Coordinator had acted in what he considered the best interests of the City.

Ryne moved through the tunnel and into the old drains with confidence. He knew his way now, and for all of his steady output of energy over many hours, he felt strong and alert. He did not hesitate when he came to the ducts and their many branchings. The schematic he had studied for so long was clear in his mind. He went directly to Warden Central. He stopped at the doorway to the guardroom, the doorway he had staggered through so long ago, and considered his next move. Drawing a stick of explosive powder from the saddlebag slung over his shoulder, he held it in one hand and took a match from his pocket with the other. Then he pushed open the door and stepped into the guardroom.

The Coordinator's face showed his weariness. His voice was thin and tired as he said to his Secretary, "Is everything ready? Have the explosion screens been issued to all the Auxiliaries?"

"Every man has one," the Secretary said. "The Wardens are getting those for their vehicles now. They should have them installed before morning."

"That's when they'll move." the Coordinator said. "They'll try to use the morning shift change to cover themselves. They'll hope to surprise us before we realize that the crowds in the streets just aren't workers changing shifts."

He leaned forward, tapping his finger on the desk top for emphasis. "Are the instructions clearly understood? Laszlo's men from the Out are to be taken into custody; they are not to be harmed. The same applies to Ryne. He is to be brought directly to me. Make sure that the

Wardens understand what I want, and that they know the penalty for failure."

"They understand," the Secretary said. "And they'll follow orders exactly." His smile was frosty. "No Warden wants to be demoted to Lower status. Even if he could stand the life, he wouldn't last long with the Bully Boys."

"Tell them again to watch especially for Ryne. He's the dangerous one."

The Secretary frowned. "You have the girl Linne in detention. Ryne won't dare cause much trouble."

The Coordinator shook his head. "One reason why you remain a Secretary is that you constantly make that kind of assumption. Ryne is dangerous because he thinks."

He tapped the desk again. "Do you remember what Amso's latest message said about Ryne's attitude toward Linne?"

"He doesn't seem as concerned about rescuing her as he was originally," the Secretary said. "Of course, this may well be due to the woman Tara's influence."

"It may well be a cover-up to lull us too," the Coordinator said tartly. He studied the Secretary closely. "Don't let yourself be fooled, man. There's a penalty for failure."

His hand slapped explosively on the desk top. "I've devoted my life to this job. My reward won't be trivial— to live in the High and see my children raised as Highs, that's something to strive for. Nor will your reward be small—if we succeed.

"Just remember that the price of failure is more than a withholding of our rewards. It will mean demotion, complete demotion. Now go contact Amso again. Find out the current situation in the Out."

The Secretary moved quietly away. He was back within minutes, his face ashen. "There is no signal. The line is dead."

"Ah," the Coordinator said. "Ryne is on his way then. Tell the Wardens to prepare themselves."

The guardroom was empty. Ryne stared into the silence, and the wrongness of this hackled the hair at the nape of his neck. Still holding the explosive stick and the match, he moved to the door leading to the street. It was unlocked. Grinning a little, he snapped the lock over and then turned to the other door, the one leading into the heart of Warden Central itself.

Here was a weakness in his plan, an area with a low success probability factor. With the hand that held the match, he eased back the door latch. Putting his foot to the panel, he kicked. The door slammed open and back against a wall. The stuffy odor of Warden Central, a combination of the stench of Lower City and of a jail, flooded over him. The banging of the door echoed hollowly through emptiness. The corridor he stared down was as deserted as the room behind him.

Again the wrongness rippled through Ryne. But he stepped into the corridor, hoping that his luck was in, that the Wardens were all out on duty. He knew it to be a futile hope before he was halfway along the corridor. Side doors opened behind and ahead of him. Men stepped out, their charged clubs held at the ready.

A dough-faced man in the uniform of a Group Officer said, "We've been waiting for you, Ryne. The Coordinator wants to see you."

Ryne put his back to the wall and held the head of the match against its rough surface. "Alive, or does it matter?"

"Alive," the dough-faced man said. "Put that match away. Nothing is going to happen to you."

"No," Ryne said. His eyes swept over the Wardens. There were eight, and none of them seemed inclined to come near him at the moment. His hope lifted slightly. That could only mean they hadn't yet been equipped with whatever anti-explosive protection the Coordinator would have had devised.

"I didn't come here to give myself up," Ryne said. "I came to borrow a remote-control communicator."

The dough-faced man shook his head. "You can't get us all—not every Warden in the building. Give up quietly." His smile was unpleasant. "The Coordinator didn't say how alive you had to be when you get to him."

Ryne touched the saddlebag. "I have this full of explosive sticks. I can light and throw them pretty fast. I've been practicing. If you don't think I can get every Warden in the building—and the building too—just try rushing me."

"Don't be a fool. You wouldn't live either."

"A damn lot of good that'll do you," Ryne said softly.

Three of the Wardens backed toward the doors they had come out of. A flicker of movement at the left caught Ryne's attention. His head swung quickly that way and then back toward the dough-faced man. "Tell the one on my left that if he throws that riot club I'll personally throw the first stick right in his face."

The dough-faced man lifted a hand. Ryne glanced to the side again. The eager Warden lowered the charged club he had poised for throwing. "What do you want a communicator for?"

"To talk with the Coordinator," Ryne said.

"You can do that from my office. I'll guarantee you safe passage."

"Passage there and back out?" Ryne mocked.

The dough-faced man licked his lips. "Listen to reason, Ryne. Our orders are to bring you in. The penalty for failure is demotion to Lower status. We might as well risk being blown up. It'll be a quicker death."

"You won't have any trouble," Ryne said. "Once the gates are open, you can go along with the rest. There'll be room for everyone in the new City."

"You haven't a chance in hell of winning," the dough-faced man said. "The Coordinator has everything taken care of."

"I know," Ryne said. "When the Lowers start toward the gate area, the Auxiliaries will show up with explosive protectors." He smiled. "Get me that communicator and you'll see who's going to win."

The dough-faced man shook his head. Ryne remained motionless. It was a stalemate. He couldn't use the explosive sticks in here without blowing himself up along with the Wardens. If they tried to take him, he would have to risk fighting them with his hands. And his chances of succeeding against eight trained men with charged riot clubs was minuscule.

He had no choice but to say, "Get me the communicator. You can listen to the conversation." He saw the slow shaking of the dough-faced man's head, and he realized that the officer knew what Ryne's chances were.

Pulling himself away from the wall, Ryne made a sudden, diving run for the door to the guardroom. He went swiftly, swinging the loaded saddlebag back and forth in front of himself. He felt the thud of it against a club and heard the soggy sound as the leather hit a Warden in the face. Then the door was directly ahead of him. He spun around, bringing the saddlebag up in a looping motion against the Warden almost up to him.

A club whistled by his head and clattered against the door. Ryne put a foot on it. With the door at his back and only six Wardens on their feet, he felt a little safer. He put the match head at the door panel. "Back up," he said. "I can light this stick and throw it and get through the door before the explosion. None of you could make it."

"You're wasting everybody's time, Ryne. The guardroom is full of my men now."

"No," Ryne said. "I locked the door to the street. They'd have to break it down, and we'd have heard that much noise. Now get me the communicator."

The dough-faced man's shoulders sagged. "Get a remote," he said to the man nearest him. He nodded and moved quickly off.

The others stood in silence except for the scuffling of feet as Ryne waved them well back from him. The Warden who had been sent away was gone over ten minutes. When he finally returned, Ryne saw his face muscles twitch as he handed the communicator to the dough-faced man.

Ryne said, "You turn it on and get the Coordinator first."

"And admit my failure personally?"

"All right," Ryne said, "then just turn it on."

The dough-faced man said wearily, "Go get another one."

The Warden moved away. Ryne called, "One that isn't booby-trapped this time." He smiled at the dough-faced man. "Your workers are sloppy. I could short the battery to the case and hook in the on-switch to give the user a knockout shock in a lot less than ten minutes."

"You can't blame me for trying," the man said.

"I can blame you for a lot of things," Ryne said. "Every one of you was a Lower. You sold yourselves for full bellies and the right to use force against other people.

And there isn't a one of you who won't jump to the other side if you see it winning."

No one answered him. The Warden returned with a communicator and again handed it to the dough-faced man. Ryne said, "Turn it on and contact the Coordinator."

The dough-faced man did so. He said, "This is Qualey at Warden Central. Ryne wants to talk to the Coordinator. Ah. Yes, he's here."

He looked at Ryne and nodded. Ryne said, "Come closer and slide it along the floor to my feet. And don't be heroic."

Qualey did as he was ordered. He stepped back to join the Wardens. Ryne bent and picked up the communicator. He had an awkward moment while he was slipping the holding strap around his neck, but none of them took advantage of his hands being occupied. Straightening up, he again put the match to the door panel.

"This is Ryne."

"So I understand. What do you want?"

Ryne said pleasantly, "A swap, Coordinator. You deliver Linne to me—alive and well—and then you come personally to Lower City and see that the big gates are open. Leave your Auxiliaries behind and order the Wardens to stay back."

"A swap," the Coordinator said. "I do all this in exchange for what from you?"

"For my guarantee not to destroy the City," Ryne said.

"Don't try to bluff me, Ryne. You don't know the game well enough."

"But I do," Ryne said quietly. "I'm going to Utilities Central right now. I have a large bag filled with explosive sticks. I know how to get below the radiation shield in the Core. What do you think will happen when I send a bagful of explosives down into the heart of the core, timed to go off when they reach the heart of the system?"

"You crazy fool! You'll destroy the City! You'll kill us all—yourself and your Linne included."

"Yes," Ryne said. "All of us—Lowers and Uppers and Highs. And it's not a bluff. I'll call from Utilities Central. I want your decision by then."

"Wait," the Coordinator said. "We can compromise. I

can see that the Lowers get more privileges, better food, more like we have up here. We don't have to destroy our entire world, Ryne."

"No," Ryne said. "I gave you my terms. I'll call in fifteen minutes for your answer."

Without closing the communicator, he reached out, opened the door to the guardroom, and stepped through. He slammed the door and locked it. The room was as empty as before, and he crossed quickly to the opening to the duct and ducked inside.

He was shaking now, fighting to retain control of himself and, at the same time, to hurry. He thought of the Coordinator. He felt a little sick. His words were irretrievable. He had made up his mind to this course of action on his way here. If the Coordinator refused to compromise, Ryne would light the long fuse and send the loaded saddlebag down into the core.

He hoped the Coordinator understood that he wasn't bluffing.

XVIII

—————

When Ryne reached the entrance to the duct that would lead him to Utilities Central, Mabton blocked his way. "You're going in the wrong direction for Upper City," he said sourly.

Ryne said, "I just made an offer to the Coordinator." He held up the portable communicator. "The Wardens were kind enough to lend it to me."

"Why shouldn't they be?" Mabton demanded.

"The first one they tried to give me was booby-trapped to stun-shock the user," Ryne said. "But with this—" he opened his saddlebag and took out an explosive stick— "they got more cooperative."

"What the hell are you trying to say?" Mabton snapped. "And just put that away. I've got some of my own." He showed Ryne a fused explosive stick and the match he held cupped in the other hand. "So just drop that bag and start for the Out," he said. "We're too close to let you cheat us now."

Ryne said wearily, "Who made you believe I was the big bad bogeyman?" He saw that the allusion was lost on Mabton; he hadn't read his fairy tales as a child. "I built the new City."

"I know that. I know why. Tara told me."

"Tara would have a good explanation," Ryne said thinly. "Did she also tell you that I would find Amso in the cave—trying to blow up the machine?" Mabton said nothing, and Ryne went on. "He followed me after I ran the machine to the valley where I built the new City. He has a communication hook-up direct to the Coordinator.

134

He's the one who's kept the Coordinator one move ahead of us."

"Don't add lying to the rest of what you've done," Mabton said.

Ryne said, "I'll tell you the same thing I told Laszlo earlier tonight. The Coordinator's known for a long time every move you've made. He knew long before I ever showed up."

Mabton said stiffly, "Keep on talking."

"I cut the communication line on my way in here tonight," Ryne said. "It wasn't too hard to find. I wonder why you didn't suspect what was happening and look for it before?"

"What the hell reason would I have had?"

"Laszlo kept telling everyone that there was a spy at the Farm and that someone was communicating with the Coordinator," Ryne reminded him.

"Laszlo doesn't know what he's saying half the time."

"And who put that idea in our minds, Mabton?" Ryne demanded. "In this case, Laszlo happened to be right. Amso was running the communicator, and Tara was feeding him the information." He saw Mabton's disbelief and he added, "Did you ever add up the time she went over there to buy cream, Mabton?"

Mabton's head swiveled briefly. "Tara, is that true?"

She came out of shadow to stare at Ryne. The magnificent autocratic beauty of her hit him as strongly as if Mabton had stepped forward and kicked him in the groin. She was behind Mabton so that he could not see her expression. But it was naked and open for Ryne's eyes.

"That's a cheap, shoddy way of trying to shift the blame," she said.

"Ask Amso," Ryne said. He took a deep breath. "Ask the Coordinator." With a flick of his thumb he opened the communicator. "Coordinator, this is Ryne. I'm waiting for your decision."

He raised the volume so that Mabton and Tara could hear. Neither of them moved as the Coordinator said, "You're bluffing, Ryne. You wouldn't destroy the City and everyone in it."

"I gave you my terms," Ryne said. "I haven't changed them."

"What would you gain?" the Coordinator demanded. "Is a principle worth your life—Linne's life? The life of the thousands in the City?"

"The Lowers won't be any worse off," Ryne said thinly. "The rest of you aren't worth saving. I gave you time enough to make your decision. If your answer is no, then I'll get to work. You can expect results within the half hour."

"Wait," the Coordinator said. "Wait. I need time to think."

"No more time," Ryne said. "And don't waste your efforts in trying to get Wardens or Auxiliaries down here to stop me. I'm at Utilities Central now." He paused and then added, "Mabton and Tara are with me. Do you want to talk to her?"

Tara jerked as if Ryne had slapped her. She made a strange, half-strangled noise and Mabton turned to look at her expression. The Coordinator said, "Tara, is he bluffing?"

She said, "No, he isn't bluffing."

"Stop him then," he shouted. "Everything is moving here. The shift change is beginning in Lower City. In an hour everything will be under control. Stop Ryne!"

Mabton screamed, "Bitch!" She tackled him. They went to the floor of the duct together, rolling wildly. Tara displayed greater strength and agility than Ryne had believed she had, and for a few moments it looked as if she might knock the small man unconscious and take the explosive stick away from him. But suddenly Mabton heaved his wiry body, sending her staggering up. He rose and rushed at her, driving his shoulder into her midriff so that she struck hard against the side of the duct. With a whimper, she collapsed and sat with her head hanging.

Ryne said, "That was your error, Coordinator. Never panic. Tara isn't a factor any more."

Mabton said, "Whatever it is Ryne said he'd do, we're doing together—now, Coordinator."

The silence was heavy, and it seemed to Ryne interminable. Finally the Coordinator said, "State your terms again, Ryne."

"Deliver Linne to me here—alive and well and unguarded. Then you come to Lower City and see that the gates are open. Leave your Auxiliaries behind and order the Wardens to stand back. Their job will be to keep the Bully Boys quiet."

"It will take time."

"Fifteen minutes," Ryne said. "I've done it through the ducts in little more time than that. Fifteen minutes, Coordinator."

He cut the circuit and put the communicator away. Mabton said, "What in the devil did you tell him you were going to do?"

Ryne stepped past Tara. "Bring her along. I'll show you."

He waited while Mabton used Tara's own belt to tie her hands loosely behind her back. Then he led the way into the great cylinder beneath the cover of Utilities Central. They stood on a spidery catwalk and stared downward as Ryne flashed his light into the depths below. The mass of cables was fused into a single great snake that went blackly downward. It reached a convex cover of some dully shining material, burrowed through it, and disappeared.

"The radiation shield," Ryne said.

"I know," Mabton said. "We talked about it before."

"I know how to get beneath it," Ryne said.

"Sure, and how long would you live?"

Ryne shrugged. "I don't know. I'm not sure what radiation is or does. But I'd live long enough to drop this sack of explosive sticks with a long fuse down into the Core."

"My God, man, you could blow . . ." Mabton stopped. "That was what you threatened to do if the Coordinator didn't meet your terms?"

"Yes," Ryne said.

Mabton laughed. "And he believed you! He didn't think you were bluffing!"

Ryne said, "Tara doesn't think so either, do you Tara?"

She lifted her head. "No," she said. "I learned a lot about Ryne lately. He doesn't bluff. He lied to me about feeling indifferent toward Linne. That was to trap me. I was fool enough to be taken in."

Mabton said savagely, "We were fools for a long time, letting you spy on us!"

"We all do what we think is right," Tara said. "I

believe in the system we have now. I risked my life to preserve it—and lost."

"You haven't lost it yet," Ryne said. "The Coordinator still has a few minutes." He nodded to Mabton. "Can you go up on the cover and watch? I want to know when Linne comes, and if the Coordinator is trying any tricks. And then we want to make sure the gates are opened and that the Lowers are allowed to leave without trouble."

"And what will you be doing?"

Ryne said, "Waiting here. In case I have to get beneath the shield and drop this bag."

"You weren't bluffing!" Mabton said. His laugh was tight. "If the Coordinator doesn't come, he's going to have a lot of company—in whatever hell he ends up."

"Lots of company," Ryne agreed. "A whole civilization for company."

He stood with Tara beside him, waiting for word from Mabton. Tara said once, "Ryne, maybe I can explain . . ."

"There's no need," he said. "You followed your beliefs; I followed mine. We both can't be right."

"But does this—whatever happens—prove who's right?"

"We'll never know," Ryne said, "but maybe your children or their children will."

"If there are any."

"Yes, if there are any." He paused a moment and said, "Maybe I'm not right, but I can't be as wrong as you and the Coordinator. I was a Lower. I know what it means to live like they do. You spent enough time in Lower City; you should understand how I feel."

"I have my own people to think about," she said. "I knew what Laszlo's plans were when he was exiled from the City. I went to the Coordinator and warned him. I told him that Laszlo and I had been close, and we agreed that I should do what I did."

"You tried to keep thousands of people in slavery, on the edge of starvation, to guarantee comforts for your own handful of people!"

"No," she said. "I tried to keep the system alive. It's my system. It isn't perfect, but for me and my people, it's better than any system Laszlo or you or any of these others could create."

Ryne said quietly, "One way or another, it's a system you'll never know again."

Before Tara could answer him, Mabton's voice came down to them. "Linne is coming. The Coordinator is with her."

"Are they alone?" Ryne demanded. He glanced up toward the opening where light outlined Mabton's head, and he glanced downward, at the dull reflection of the radiation cover.

"I can't tell yet," Mabton called back.

Ryne leaned over, looking downward, wondering what he would do if the Coordinator refused to follow instructions, wondering just how he could break through that radiation cover.

And then Tara jumped striking his back with her shoulder, using her strength and weight to send him over the edge of the catwalk and down onto the dully shining metal radiation shield.

XIX

As he felt himself overbalancing on the edge of the catwalk, Ryne threw the saddlebag in desperation at the corner stanchion. He felt the thick strap take hold and stop his fall with one boot tip still on the catwalk.

Tara came awkwardly at him, jumping because of the rope hobbling her ankles. With her hands tied behind her back, she had no choice but to lie down and kick out at his boot with her feet. Ryne felt the strain on his back and shoulders as he swung out and away. He wondered how much weight the strap could take, and then he had one hand on the stanchion. With another swing, he planted his feet on the end of the catwalk and pulled himself back to safety.

Tara lay crying on the catwalk where she had thrown herself. Suddenly she began to hump forward. Ryne reached her just as the weight of her legs and hips began to carry her over the edge. His hands caught her under the armpits and he jerked her savagely back. Swinging her around, he pushed her against the stanchion. He tied her there.

"No," he said. "You can't get out of your debt that cheaply."

He turned and called again, "Mabton, are they alone?"

After a moment's silence, Mabton said, "They're alone. Just Linne and the Coordinator."

"Have him send her up to the top. There should be a ladder from the floor on the side facing the door."

Ryne turned to Tara and released the rope holding her to the stanchion. Using it as he would a pair of reins for a horse, he herded her back into the duct and then up to the top of the great cylinder. The heavy saddlebag slapped against his hip as he walked, and once he stopped to put a hand gratefully on it.

They went in silence to where Mabton waited. He looked curiously at Tara's tear-streaked face and then at Ryne as he untied her ankle and wrist ropes. "You trust her?"

Ryne said dryly, "I prefer her down with the Coordinator."

Ryne moved to the rim of the cylinder and looked down into the gloom of the vast room. Light from the doorway outlined the Coordinator standing motionless. Ryne could not see Linne without leaning far over, but he could hear her steady progress up the ladder.

Then her head appeared and in a moment she was caught in his arms. He said, "You're all right?"

"I am now. I'm fine."

She was trembling. He kissed her gently. She stepped back, touching his face with her fingertips. Her eyes moved to Mabton and then on to Tara. "That's the High woman?"

"Yes," Ryne said. "Tara, go join your boss."

She threw back her head and laughed at him. "My boss! I'm the boss, Ryne. Didn't you know that? I'm a High. The Coordinator works for me."

"Then," Ryne said quietly, "go tell him to finish carrying out our agreement."

She scrambled down the ladder. Once she was well out of Ryne's reach, she called, "I forbid you to do this! You had no right to give in to Ryne!"

"I had the right to save the City," he said. "You said yourself that Ryne wasn't bluffing."

"There isn't a High living who wouldn't rather be dead than have to live and work in this filth!" she screamed at him.

The Coordinator was as suave and calm as ever. "There are more Uppers than Highs to consider. Besides, it's too late. I already gave the orders. The Auxiliaries are still in Upper City. The Wardens' only job is to arrest the Bully Boys."

"Arrest them!"

"Of course," he said equably. "Do you think I want animals like that living with me?"

"I'll ruin you for this!" Tara cried imperiously. "You're still under my orders."

"There's nothing you can do to me that my failure hasn't already done," he said. He started out.

Ryne said, "Wait. Mabton is going with you—to observe." He turned to Mabton. "Once you're sure everything is under control, come and get me." He touched Linne. "Go with Mabton and leave with the others."

"And you?"

"I'm staying. It isn't too late for the Coordinator to try one of his tricks on us." He held up the bag of explosive sticks. "Coordinator, I still have this. Remember that."

"There won't be any trouble," the Coordinator said. He stepped aside as Tara came up to him, lifted a hand, and then dropped it to rush into the street.

Mabton started down the ladder, stopped and looked back. Linne said, "I'm staying with Ryne. When we leave, we'll do it together."

Mabton went on, and in a moment he and the Coordinator moved outside together. Ryne led Linne to the side of the core. They sat down beside one another, their backs to the wall.

"I'm not going to leave you again," she said softly. Her quizical smile touched him. "The Coordinator told me that you and Tara had a pair-up."

"No," Ryne said. "We were together, alone, a few nights. Nothing more than that." He explained the circumstances to her briefly.

She said, as if satisfying herself with an explanation, "You suspected her even then. I suppose that's the best way to gain a woman's confidence—through her emotions."

"She was trying to use me," Ryne said.

"But you used her instead," Linne said. She rubbed her shoulder against his. "I think you're very clever, Ryne."

He laughed a little, very softly. He wasn't really sure whether he was lying by agreeing with her or whether the idea had been in the back of his mind all along. He decided it was not a thing to discuss with her.

When Mabton returned, they descended to the floor and followed him onto the street. Lower City was empty and silent. When they reached the gates, only a few stragglers were passing through. They moved hesitantly, gingerly from the protection of the City to the unknown Out. Weir and Corso were at one side, watching them, and giving words of encouragement. Near Weir the Coordinator stood with shoulders sagging and head bowed in defeat.

As Ryne passed, the Coordinator looked up. "I'm glad you left. If you'd stayed on my side, you'd have ended up taking my place and running the City."

"If I were you, I'd worry about Tara doing just that," Ryne said. "She lost her balance today, but watch out when she gets it back."

"I intend to," the Coordinator said dryly. "I've already got a nice factory job picked out for her."

Ryne and Linne walked on, through the gates and into the Out. The glow coming through the new force dome was visible above the bulk of the nearest hill. Both moons came gamboling across the sky, throwing light enough for the long line of people to see easily as they followed the path over the hill and down to the valley of the new City.

Numerical Checklist of DAW BOOKS
NEVER BEFORE IN PAPERBACK

UQ1001	SPELL OF THE WITCH WORLD by Andre Norton	
UQ1002	THE MIND BEHIND THE EYE by Joseph Green	
UQ1003	THE PROBABILITY MAN by Brian N. Ball	
UQ1004	THE BOOK OF VAN VOGT	
UQ1005	THE 1972 ANNUAL WORLD'S BEST SF	
UQ1006	THE DAY STAR by Mark Geston	
UQ1007	TO CHALLENGE CHAOS by Brian M. Stableford	
UQ1008	THE MINDBLOCKED MAN by Jeff Sutton	
UQ1009	TACTICS OF MISTAKE by Gordon R. Dickson	
UQ1010	AT THE SEVENTH LEVEL by Suzette Haden Elgin	
UQ1011	THE DAY BEFORE TOMORROW by Gerard Klein	
UQ1012	A DARKNESS IN MY SOUL by Dean R. Koontz	
UQ1013	THE YEAR'S BEST HORROR STORIES	
UQ1014	WE CAN BUILD YOU by Philip K. Dick	
UQ1015	THE WORLD MENDERS by Lloyd Biggle, Jr.	
UQ1016	GENIUS UNLIMITED by John T. Phillifent	
UQ1017	BLUE FACE by G. C. Edmondson	
UQ1018	CENTURY OF THE MANIKIN by E. C. Tubb	
UQ1019	THE REGIMENTS OF NIGHT by Brian N. Ball	
UQ1020	OLE DOC METHUSELAH by L. Ron Hubbard	
UQ1021	DINOSAUR BEACH by Keith Laumer	
UQ1022	THE RETURN OF THE TIME MACHINE by Egon Friedell	
UQ1023	THE STARDROPPERS by John Brunner	
UQ1024	THE CITY MACHINE by Louis Trimble	

All DAW books are 95¢ (plus 15¢ postage & handling if by mail)

Four new SF books each month by the best of the SF authors. Ask your favorite local paperback book shop or newsdealer for DAW BOOKS.

DAW BOOKS are represented by the publishers of Signet and Mentor Books, THE NEW AMERICAN LIBRARY, INC.